Cupcakes & Curses

A Paranormal Cozy Mystery

Jane Hinchey

Baywolf Press

By Jane Hinchey

Witch Way to Murder & Mayhem

Witch Way to Romance & Ruin

Witch Way Down Under

Witch Way to Beauty & the Beach

Witch Way to Death & Destruction

Witch Way to Secrets & Sorcery

Ghost Mortem

Give up the Ghost

The Ghost is Clear

A Ghost of a Chance

ISBN: 978-1-922745-00-2

Baywolf Press

PO Box 43, Ingle Farm, SA, 5098

Australia

www.baywolfpress.com

About this Book

The guest list for the shifter party Kristina Gates is catering has just turned into a suspect list—for murder.

When Ted McNeil is found dead at a high society event, it looks at first like he choked on one of Kristina's cupcakes. But it soon becomes evident that foul play was involved. The cupcake was poisoned.

Kristina's determination to salvage her reputation and learn the truth launches her quest to appease the Witches' Council and avoid a life sentence in the pokey. With the help of her fae friends and sexy Watcher Ben Hoffman, she untangles a web of lies that threaten her very existence.

Faced with a mysterious foe, a family of tight-lipped shifters, and a competitor who would stop at nothing to put her out of business, Kristina realizes nothing is as it seems and the shadows hold secrets that some would kill to keep.

'Cupcakes & Curses' is a stand-alone paranormal cozy mystery. If you like colorful whodunnits, supernatural intrigue, and murders paired with sweet desserts, then you'll love this quick read.

Chapter One

"**I** spent two weeks perfecting that spell. Now I wish I hadn't."

Velma didn't respond—not so much as a meow. I glanced at her where she sat on the corner of my kitchen counter, watching the wooden spoon as it rotated around and around in the bowl by itself. I flicked my fingers and the spoon stopped. Velma looked at me, eyes accusing. Her ear twitched and I bit back a smile.

The spell had been a special request from Katherine Quinn, a cougar shifter and one of

Redmeadows elite. Katherine and her family came from old money, so when she rang requesting that you cater an informal soirée for her son, Wes, and that you also infuse the dessert cupcakes with something extra special, you didn't argue. Katherine had wanted her guests infused with love and acceptance. A tough one. Too much love and it would tip into lust, and then you'd have people making out with random strangers. I knew because I'd tested the first batch in my shop, with disastrous results. I'd had to counteract the spell, settling instead for happiness and acceptance, and then tweak it to find the right level of both.

What I hadn't expected was for one of Katherine's guests to choke on a cupcake. Ted McNeil had been Wes's best friend. He'd been wolfing down one of my creations when he turned blue in the face, clutched his throat, and keeled over. Even my magic couldn't save him. Katherine and Wes had proceeded to call the authorities and soothe their spooked guests, keeping them calm. I couldn't say I would have acted the same if I had been in their shoes. If someone dropped dead at my party, I'd be freaking out big time. I shrugged —just went to show I was totally out of their league.

Ruffling Velma behind the ears, I set the wooden spoon to stirring again. I needed more good luck brownies for my coffee shop, Jam, along with another two dozen confidence cookies that were now baking in the oven.

"Meow."

"What is it, girl?"

The doorbell chimed. Velma had the uncanny ability to predict whenever someone was about to ring the damn thing. She hated interruptions as much as I did. She jumped down from the counter as I wiped my flour-covered hands on my jeans and headed for the front door. I waited until Velma had disappeared upstairs before opening it.

"Yes?" Before me towered a God. Or as near as. Over six feet of very well put-together male stood on my front step, dark hair tousled as if he'd run his fingers through it countless times, five o'clock shadow dusting his chiseled jaw. I mean, he was a cliché on legs, and I didn't mind admitting that just the sight of him did funny things to my insides.

"Kristina Gates?" One dark brow arched over eyes as black as night.

"Who's asking?" I leaned against the door frame, folding my arms across my chest to stop myself from reaching out and running my fingers over his pecs. And abs. He had to have rock-hard abs under that black T-shirt he wore, right?

I blinked at the badge he suddenly thrust in my face. A Watcher from the Council. Well, that was unexpected.

"Watcher Ben Hoffman. Can I have a word?"

"Sure."

"Can I come in?"

I heaved a sigh, turning inside. "I guess."

I heard the front door close and could feel the heat of his body as he followed close behind. I turned into the living area, sending a quick flick of magic to halt the spoon stirring in the kitchen.

"Have a seat." I indicated the sofa while I perched on one of the mismatched armchairs. "So what does the Council want with little old me?"

"I'm investigating the death of Ted McNeil. Know him?" he asked.

"I do." The guy who'd choked on my cupcake. I guess I should have expected some sort of investigation, but after I'd given my statement to the police yesterday, I'd been free to go, and I hadn't expected any further questioning, let alone from a Watcher.

"But…he was human, right? Why is a Watcher investigating?" I clutched a hand to my throat. "Is it because of me? My cupcakes had magic, is that why?"

"I'll ask the questions if you don't mind." His face was impassive as he pulled out his phone and flicked through the screen. He scanned the contents, then looked back at me.

"You were hired by Katherine Quinn to cater the party she held yesterday in Adelaide Park?"

"She hired me to cater the dessert buffet, yes. The savory side of things was handled by another caterer."

"Yes, right, I have that here." Ben scrolled through his screen again. "Jodi O'Flannigan of Flans and Things."

I snickered. I'd always thought Jodi had chosen an atrocious name for her business, a play on her surname, but hey, to each her own.

"Why didn't Mrs. Quinn contract Jodi to do the dessert buffet as well?"

"I don't know. You'd have to ask her," I lied.

Ben met my eyes, his gaze drilling into me with laser precision. I got the feeling he knew I was lying. The truth was, my desserts rocked, thanks to my touch of magic. Jodi had been trying to replicate my desserts for months with no success. And that was why Katherine had hired me— because my cupcakes were magical.

"She told me the cupcakes were a special request," he continued, without calling me on the lie, which got my attention. Why would a Watcher let a lie slide? Interesting.

Velma padded into the room, winding herself around Ben's legs. He absently stroked her and she purred. My mouth fell open. Velma hated strangers and most definitely didn't allow them to stroke her, let alone offer up a purr. I frowned, examining him closely.

He noticed my scrutiny, the corner of his lip turned up in a smirk.

"Worked it out yet?" he asked.

I shook my head. Nope. He was something, all right, but I couldn't put my finger on it. Not a shifter. Definitely not a vamp. But something. The Council appointed different species as Watchers, similar to the police in human terms, so it was a given that he was some sort of paranormal. I just couldn't put my finger on what he was exactly.

"This might help." With the slightest of hand gestures, his whole body shimmered, and I saw him. The real him. Physically, he looked the same, but now I could see his magic.

"You're a witch! Or a wizard, or warlock, or whatever you guys call yourselves."

"Witch is fine."

As his words sank in, my thoughts returned to why he was here. "Why did the Council send you? While Ted's death is tragic and I feel terrible, I don't understand why choking warrants an investigation by a Watcher." The Council ruled over all paranormals. If we broke any rules, we had them to answer to. If they were looking into a human death, it could only mean one thing. Trouble.

"He didn't choke." Ben leaned back against the sofa, his sharp gaze never leaving me.

"He didn't?"

"He was poisoned."

I bit my lip. "Oh, shit."

"Exactly," he said, nodding.

"You think I did it."

"Not necessarily. But I need to ask you some questions."

My breath puffed out and I sank back into my chair, stunned. My cupcake had been poisoned. Implicating me! I bristled, on the defensive.

"I can assure you, Watcher, I did not poison my own cupcakes. I would never wish to harm another person, nor would I risk my reputation, my business."

Ignoring my passionate outburst, Ben said, "Take me through the afternoon. Step by step."

"Well...okay. The event was an afternoon tea type affair, due to start at four. I arrived at two to begin setting up. It actually didn't take me that long. I was all done by three, so I chatted with some of the wait staff—I'd met some of them before on other catering jobs. Like the Corosoes' wedding anniversary last month. That was a cracker of a night..." I trailed off, lost in the memory until he cleared his throat, bringing my attention back.

"You stay—you attend the events you cater?"

"Yes. It's good networking for my business. Once people taste my desserts, they usually have questions, and I like to inform them firsthand. Plus, I supply my own trays and cake stands, so I can pack them up and bring them home with me when we're done and not risk having them disappear into the back of another caterer's truck."

"McNeil died just after six. What were you doing between four and six, once the event started?"

"I pretty much stayed by the buffet table. It didn't get much attention until around five, five-thirty. Most people go for the savory first, then move on to dessert, but a few people who know me skipped the savory buffet and came straight to me. I spent a few minutes chatting with them, introducing them to new cupcakes they may not have tried before. Plus, I kept the cake trays well stocked and fresh. If someone swiped their finger through the icing on a cupcake, for a sneaky taste, I'd swap it out for a fresh one, that type of thing."

"People do that?"

"All the time."

"And you stayed at the dessert buffet table the entire time?" he pressed.

"I went for a toilet break at about a quarter to six or thereabouts." I shrugged. Who could remember intricate details of potty breaks?

"How long were you gone?"

"I don't know. How long does it take to pee and wash your hands? Not long."

"Did you know Ted McNeil?" He switched tack and it took me a second to catch up.

"In passing. He's been in my shop a time or two, but usually, he sends his assistant in to get his coffee." I shrugged. Ted was a big deal in the business world, but from what I'd seen, he was also a bit of a jerk.

"You haven't catered any events for him?"

"No. I believe Jodi has a catering contract with him."

"What magic did you infuse the cupcakes with? Specifically, the cupcakes with the blue butterfly icing." This time he showed me his phone, the image of my blue cupcake on the screen.

"Happiness and acceptance. All of the desserts were infused with happiness and acceptance, not just the blue butterflies."

"Why did you choose that?"

"I didn't. Katherine requested it."

"Do you know why?"

"You'll have to ask her Watcher." I shrugged. I'd thought it an unusual request, but it's not up to me to question my clients. I simply do as they ask.

"She knows you're a witch?"

"I would assume so, just as I know she's a shifter. I follow the Council rules, Watcher. I don't reveal my powers to humans."

"Yet you use magic in your cakes."

"I have permission from the Council, as long as I don't use anything that takes away free will, such as love potions. I stick to things like good luck, adrenaline, confidence, inspiration, that sort of thing." I paused. "Can I ask a question?"

"Sure."

"What was the poison?"

"Abatwa poison." He watched me, waited while recognition kicked in.

"We have Abatwa? In Redmeadows?" The Abatwa was a tiny race, so small they could hide beneath a blade of grass, but you'd be a fool to underestimate them. They were voracious eaters; a tribe of them could strip a large animal in a day. And they were very, very, sensitive about their size. Insult them, and you could find yourself on the wrong end of a poison arrow. If you were to accidentally tread on one, it would be futile to make any long-term plans, because that little poison arrow would pierce the sole of your shoe, delivering the deadly toxin.

"Wait!" I held up a hand. "I'm confused. Are you telling me Abatwa poison was in my cupcake, or that Ted was shot by an Abatwa arrow?" There was a big difference. One could clear my name, while the other would implicate me big time.

"We found trace amounts in the icing of the cupcake."

"And it was just that one cupcake?"

"We're still testing them, but yes, it appears it was only in that one cupcake."

I thought for a moment, my mind a jumble. Besides someone being able to get their hands on Abatwa poison, why poison Ted? Was he even the target, or had there been a mistake? *Good question.*

"Do you think Ted was the target, or...?"

"Most likely. For someone to go to the trouble of procuring Abatwa poison, they wouldn't waste it on a random person. This was specific and undetectable by humans. The coroner will find nothing and most likely rule his death a heart attack—he didn't choke and no food was found in his throat or airway. There were just remnants in his mouth."

"So, if it wasn't some random thing and anyone could have taken that specific cake, whoever did it had to know he'd pick that one. And they probably planted the poison just beforehand, otherwise, they would have risked not only someone else taking it, but me moving things around. I often rotate the cakes. The ones that have been out for a while get moved to the front and the fresh ones go to the back."

"Are these your cupcakes?" Ben held out his phone, an image glowing on the screen. I leaned forward and squinted at the picture. Sure enough, it showed a cake stand full of cupcakes neatly arranged. Each cake featured a different-colored butterfly, creating a rainbow of pink, blue, green, purple, and yellow.

"Yeah, they look like mine."

"It looks like a lot of work to individually decorate each cupcake like that."

"It is. But it's what I do, Watcher. I don't just bake, I create."

Ben rose, sliding the phone into the back pocket of his jeans. I stood facing him.

"So. What now?" I asked.

"I find out who did this." He grinned, holding out a card to me. "Here's my number. If you think of anything, call me. Oh, and don't leave town."

I took the card, glancing at it. "So I'm really a suspect?" The very idea set my teeth on edge.

"Everyone who attended the party is a suspect. That poison didn't get into the cupcake on its own."

"Right. That don't leave town thing—that's just a line right? A bit of a joke because that's what they say in the TV shows?"

"No joke. Why, did you have plans to be somewhere?" He cocked his head.

"Nah. Just curious. I have no plans. I'm usually here or at my shop."

He nodded. "Thanks for your time, Miss Gates."

"Call me Kristina. If you're going to be interrogating me on a regular basis, we may as well use first names. Ben." I grinned, feeling cheeky. Thankfully, he smiled back instead of slapping me in cuffs and dragging me to the Council.

Chapter Two

"Oh my God! I saw you on the news!" Paige grabbed me by the hand and dragged me into the kitchen as soon as I stepped over the threshold at Jam. Paige was my assistant manager, my best friend, and a fae. "Are you okay? How awful."

"I'm fine. Get this, I'm also a suspect!"

"What the hell? The guy choked. You can't be blamed for that." Paige stood with her legs planted, fists resting on her hips, her body vibrating with outrage on my behalf. She was such a sweetheart.

"Turns out he didn't choke. He was poisoned, but keep that to yourself okay? Although the Watcher didn't tell me not to tell anyone. Maybe I should call him to clarify." Who was I kidding? I'd drum up any excuse to call him, just to hear his deep voice in my ear, doing crazy things to my libido.

"Wait! Watcher? What Watcher?"

"Watcher Ben Hoffman. Talk about friggin' eye candy, Paige. This guy is not only built but seriously gorgeous. And a witch." My voice dropped at the end. *A witch*. What a combination.

"The Council," Paige breathed, clasping my hands, her green eyes pools of concern. "The Council is investigating you? They think you killed that guy?"

"Not necessarily. But I'm implicated because I baked the cupcakes, and they want the Watcher to keep an eye on me since he's poking around as part of his job anyway."

"Jesus, what a mess."

"I don't like it," I admitted, pulling an apron over my head and tying it behind my back. "This is my reputation that's at stake. And my freedom. If the Council thinks I did it, I'll be in the witches' pokey. I can't sit around and do nothing."

"What are you suggesting?" Paige went to the two big industrial fridges against the far wall and began pulling out the ingredients I'd need. Milk, eggs, butter.

"I want to talk to the Quinn's. They have to know something. Katherine was insistent that I infuse the desserts with love and acceptance. Did she know someone there who needed such a thing? Someone who was filled with hate that needed an emotional pick-me-up?"

"What are you making?" Paige indicated the stainless steel bench I was standing at.

"Oh, um, I'll do a batch of adrenaline coffee cake. And I did some baking at home yesterday. Can you grab the cookies and brownies from the back of the van?"

"Sure." Paige finished getting the rest of the ingredients I'd need, then left to retrieve the goodies I'd left in the van.

"Hey." Laura poked her head into the kitchen. "How are you holding up?"

"Oh, hi, Laura. Yeah, I'm fine. Thanks for asking."

Laura and her boyfriend, Cody, were my main staff. They helped me keep Jam running like a well-oiled machine. Like Paige, they were also fae. Fae were great with the customers and had a wicked sweet tooth, which explained why they were attracted to working in jobs that involved sweets and desserts. Between Paige, Laura, and Cody, I had nothing to worry about when it came to my shop. They organized staff rosters, made sure the cleaning crew were on top of things, maintained my pantry so I never ran out of anything, and passed on useful customer feedback on my creations. I wouldn't have been able to do this without them. They'd become my family.

"Ummm." Laura hesitated, and I glanced up.

"What is it?"

"The Whitfield's just canceled. You were supposed to cater their daughter's birthday party this weekend."

"Damn it." It was bound to happen. I just hadn't expected it so soon. I needed to get this whole mess resolved quickly, or it could mean the end of my business. I'd built it up through word of mouth, and word of mouth could tear it down just as quickly. Until I could clear my name, I was at risk of losing it all.

"Freeze." I waved my hand over the coffee cake in progress in front of me, holding it in suspended animation. I'd get back to it later. Right now, I needed to talk to the Quinn's and clear my name.

"I'm going out. You guys are okay here, right? I did some baking yesterday. Paige is just bringing it in. The coffee cake will have to wait, but you've plenty of stock otherwise."

"Yeah, we're good. You go, everything is fine here."

Whipping the apron off, I tossed it onto the counter and grabbed my old bomber jacket, pulling it on as I let myself out the back door of the shop. The seasons had begun to change, which meant layers. Too hot one minute—too cold the next. My usual attire of jeans and a T-shirt worked just fine, and my faded red Chucks were a daily staple, but this morning I'd had to add the jacket to keep the chill from my bones.

"Kristina! What a lovely surprise. I wasn't expecting you." Katherine Quinn rose from where she was seated at her glass dining table with an iPad in front of her and a cup and saucer at her elbow. "Thank you, Mary, that'll be all." She dismissed the young woman who'd let me in.

"Sorry for arriving unannounced," I apologized, not really sorry.

"How are you faring after yesterday's terrible events?" Katherine indicated a chair opposite her and I slid in, taking care not to touch the tabletop

and leave fingerprints. Katherine's apartment—
well, it wasn't really an apartment, since it was
bigger than most houses I knew—was beautiful.
Though every item in it was expensive, her
decorator had introduced elegance to the home
that was unpretentious. Besides the glass
tabletops, I loved it.

"Not good."

"Oh?" This got her attention. She'd gone back to
scrolling through the iPad, but now her
beautifully coiffed head snapped up and her eyes
bore into mine.

"I've already had one catering event cancel. I
fear there will be more to follow. I cannot afford
to have my name and reputation dragged through
the mud."

"Of course not, my dear, but I'm unsure how
you think I can help you. The whole unfortunate
mess is being handled by the police."

"And the Council."

A perfectly manicured brow rose. "The Council
is involved? That's...unexpected. Ted was human,

and although he moved in the same circles as a lot of paranormals, as far as I'm aware, he wasn't made privy to our existence."

"Wes never let slip that you're shifters?"

"Well..." Katherine glanced over my head, deep in thought, then brought her gaze back to mine. "Not many people know this, but Wes isn't a shifter," she admitted.

"Oh. I'd heard that could happen sometimes." Though it was rare for two shifters to not produce shifter offspring.

Katherine cut into my thoughts. "Wes is adopted. Bart and I were unable to conceive. Most likely because I'm a Cougar Shifter and he was a Wolf Shifter. We adopted Wes through human channels."

"Does Wes know?"

"Yes, Wes knows everything—that his father and I are shifters, that he's adopted and one-hundred percent human."

"That was a risk."

Katherine shrugged. "Bart and I thought it best. We didn't want secrets in our home. And I'm glad for it. Wes had a happy childhood. Losing Bart was hard on both of us, but we supported each other. We got through it together."

I nodded. Family almost always supported each other, through thick and thin. I envied Katherine that, for I hadn't known my parents. Documents had told me my mother was a witch and my father a fae. For reasons unknown to me, they gave me up at birth. I'd been raised in foster homes until I struck out on my own at eighteen, as soon as I was able to get myself out of the human tangle of bureaucracy that had dictated my life until that point. To this day I still don't know why the Council hadn't stepped in and had me placed with a paranormal family.

"I understand, and I don't expect you to help me. Just...can I ask you some questions? The Watcher has to interview everyone in attendance and that's going to take some time, time I don't have. The grapevine is vicious at times like this."

Katherine nodded. "What you say is true, my dear. Idle gossips can be a dangerous thing. Ask away. I'll do my best to answer your questions."

"Thank you." I blew out a breath. "Let's start with Ted. Do you know why someone would want him dead?"

"No, I don't. Oh, I know he wasn't well-liked in business circles, that he was thought to be cutthroat and ruthless, but to be perfectly honest, that's just business!"

"He and Wes had been friends for a long time?"

"Since grade school. They'd had their fallings-out over the years, as all boys do—usually over a girl—but they remained close and loyal friends. We considered Teddy a part of the family."

I nodded. I'd heard enough gossip to know what she said was true. Ted and Wes had grown up like brothers.

"Can I ask, when you hired me, why you requested I infuse the desserts with love and acceptance?"

"Nothing sinister my dear, I can assure you." Katherine laughed. "I wanted my guests to feel hopeful and happy. After that nasty business at the lake last month, I couldn't help but notice, at least in my circle of friends, that everyone was fearful and angry. That's no way to live life, as I'm sure you'll agree."

She was referring to the destruction of a luxury yacht on Lake Ceduna, in which seventeen people had died after a bomb went off. The culprit, it turned out, was a deckhand who had been fired the week before. Katherine was right—the mood over Redmeadows had been pretty subdued for a while, and it must've been particularly difficult for Katherine. She'd known those people.

"It was terrible," I agreed. "I'm sure the police have already asked, but did you see anything, notice anything unusual at the party? At any time?"

"No, I didn't. Just the usual. Oh, wait..."

"Yes?" I leaned forward, hopeful.

"My other caterer, Jodi O'Flannigan, spent a lot of time scowling in your direction."

I sat back in my seat. "That's nothing new."

"She was also in quite an intense conversation with another woman. Rebecca—I can't recall her last name. Wes invited a lot of guests personally, guests that he knew I wouldn't approve of." Katherine waved a hand. "Anyway, I couldn't hear what they were saying, but it looked like a disagreement of some sort. Then it looked like this Rebecca woman and Ted had words."

"So, after you saw Rebecca and Jodi talking, you then saw Rebecca and Ted...arguing?"

"I couldn't say for sure since I couldn't hear them, but there were lots of hand gestures and angry faces. That's when I stepped in and suggested Teddy might like a cupcake, knowing your special blend would alleviate all this tension. Oh!" Her hand flew to her mouth.

Oh, indeed. She'd directed Ted to the cupcakes. He'd done as she suggested and died as a result.

"Does the Watcher know this?" I asked.

"Not yet. I just remembered it while talking to you. But I'm going to call him now. Whatever was going on between Rebecca, Jodi, and Teddy, it could be important."

"Or it could be nothing." I didn't know why, but I felt the need to play devil's advocate, especially where Jodi was concerned. "Thanks for talking with me today, Katherine. I'll let myself out."

I wanted to be gone before she called the Watcher. And I wanted to chat with Jodi O'Flannigan.

Chapter Three

I was all out of luck. I'd just stepped through the door of Jodi's shop, Flans and Things, intent on having it out with the woman, when I ran smack dab into Watcher Ben Hoffman. Literally. I bounced off his broad back and nearly landed on my ass in the doorway.

"Ooof."

"Sorry. Are you okay?" Ben turned, eyes twinkling when he recognized me. "Hey."

"Hey yourself," I grumbled, embarrassed to be caught not looking where I was going. "Any reason you decided to stand right in the middle of the doorway?" Straight on the offensive. Good one, I chided myself.

"I'm not. Well, not intentionally. I'm in the queue." He moved aside so I could see the line of customers waiting to be served. Flans and Things was hopping.

"Checking out the competition?" he inquired, doing that one eyebrow arch thing that I could never pull off. How did he operate his eyebrows independent of each other? Whenever I tried it, both my brows practically disappeared into my hairline.

"Hardly," I scoffed. I spied Jodi through the pass-through hatch, busy in the kitchen. Doubtful she'd take time out to talk to me, not with a shop full of hungry customers. A little voice in the back of my head reminded me that she probably wouldn't talk with me anyway, busy or not.

"I had an interesting conversation with Mrs. Quinn." Ben folded his arms across that impressive chest of his and looked down at me.

Not out of disapproval, but because of his height. I craned my neck to try and stare him down. It didn't work. He was on to me, judging by the twitch of his lip.

"Oh?" I feigned ignorance.

"She told me you'd dropped by, were having a little chat when she remembered Jodi, Ted, and a woman named Rebecca involved in some sort of argument."

"You probably shouldn't be telling me that," I scolded, "Isn't it part of your investigation? I'm sure the Council frowns on revealing details of an ongoing investigation, let alone the source."

"Since you already know, because you were there, I'm not breaking any rules. At least that makes one of us."

"What are you insinuating?" My hand pressed to my chest in mock innocence. I knew exactly what he was getting at.

"That you're poking your nose where it doesn't belong. Leave the Watcher work to me. You know. Since I'm a Watcher and all."

"You don't understand." I reached out, clutching his arm. "I've already had a catering job cancel this morning. More are going to follow. The longer it takes to get to the truth, the more my business will suffer. And it's not just me I'm worried about. If my business fails, so does the livelihood of my staff. I didn't do this. I need to clear my name!"

Ben frowned at me, concern evident on his oh-so-handsome face. Man, he was gorgeous. And a distraction.

"We will get to the bottom of it. Don't worry."

"Pfft. 'Don't worry,' he says. You'll still have a paycheck rolling in, no matter the outcome. This is my life on the line."

"Er, bit dramatic don't you think? Your life isn't at risk, Kristina. Unless there's something you're not telling me? Have threats been made?" Suddenly he was in Watcher mode, body ramrod straight, eyes drilling into me, all signs of teasing gone.

"No. Nothing like that. I just can't sit on my hands and do nothing," I huffed.

He had me. I was being overly dramatic, I knew it, he knew it. My cheeks heating with embarrassment, I spun on my heel and exited the shop. I'd have to hunt Jodi down later—it had been a long shot to get her to talk to me anyway, and even if she agreed, could I trust anything she'd tell me? I was two steps down the footpath when a strong hand grasped my upper arm, halting me.

"Wait."

"What?" I was irritated. At myself. At him. At the cards I'd been dealt.

"I know you want this solved…"

I cut him off. "Damn straight I do!"

"But," he continued as if I hadn't spoken, "this is a homicide, Kristina. Someone got murdered. It's dangerous. If you start poking your nose where it's not wanted, well, let's just say you don't want to get in this person's crosshairs."

"So you're saying now is not the time to develop my amateur sleuthing skills?"

He nodded, face grim. "That's exactly what I'm saying."

I sighed.

"Fine," I huffed, tugging my arm out of his grip and continuing down the sidewalk. He didn't need to know I had no intention of stopping.

At the corner, I cast a glance over my shoulder. He stood there, feet planted a shoulder-width apart, eyes on me. My hormones flared to life, and I bit my lip. Man, why did he have to be so goddamn gorgeous? And nice? He was really going to be pissed at me, and that was a shame because I liked him.

Remembering the half-prepared coffee cake at Jam, I returned to my shop. I was heartened to see all the tables full.

"Lost another," Paige told me as I waved my hand over the cake mixture, unfreezing it. The wooden spoon began to lazily stir the batter as I sprinkled in ingredients. I didn't use fancy food processors or beaters. I made everything by hand.

Okay, fine—by magic.

"Who?"

"The Meyer engagement party."

"Damn it. They were new, we could've really broadened our reach with them."

Paige's face fell, and I felt bad. This wasn't their fault, nor should it be their problem. "It'll be okay," I said. "The Watcher is making progress, and look, the shop is full. Our regulars who know and love us won't abandon us."

Paige nodded, a smile flitting across her face. "They're great, aren't they?"

"They are amazing. And with a couple of cancellations, that gives me some spare time."

"Spare time to catch a killer?"

"Well, I told the Watcher I wouldn't," I admitted.

"Ha. And he believed you?" Paige snorted.

"Probably not."

With a shrug, I pulled my tattered notebook out from under the counter. This was my work-in-progress book. I used it to play with new recipes. I'd started planning a blueberry muffin that I wanted to infuse with optimism. The first batch had tasted awful, but I definitely felt optimistic after taking a bite. I also had a strawberry cheesecake that I wanted to infuse with a sense of summer—the holiday vibe, long, hot days at the beach, sipping cocktails with the person you like most in the world by your side. With these cancellations, I had more time to spend on my new creations.

"Do you know a woman named Rebecca?" I asked Paige as I thumbed through my notebook.

"I know a couple of Rebecca's. You're going to have to give me a little more to go on."

I laughed. Of course, there were multiple Rebecca's in Redmeadows. Duh. "All I know is that a woman named Rebecca was arguing with both Jodi and Ted yesterday at the afternoon tea.

I'm wondering who she is. And how I can go about finding her."

"Ah, well, no, I can't help you. The Rebecca's I know would never have been invited to a high society event like the Quinn's afternoon tea. Do you have a description?"

"Shit. I don't. I'm such an idiot. I should have asked Mrs. Quinn for one, but I didn't. She was intent on ringing the Watcher and I bolted."

"Mrs. Quinn called the Watcher on you?"

"No. She remembered the argument when we were talking. She wanted to share the info with the Watcher. And I didn't want to get busted, so I high-tailed it out of there."

"I'm guessing you got busted anyway?"

"Big time. I went to see Jodi, and who do I run into? Watcher Ben Hoffman. And he'd already spoken with Mrs. Quinn."

"Was he awful to you?" Paige said sympathetically.

"The opposite. He was really nice, but insistent that I stop poking around. For my own safety."

"He thinks you're in danger?" Paige gasped, hand at her throat.

"Not really. He just pointed out that someone murdered Ted. If that someone discovers I'm poking around—and possibly getting close to revealing their identity—well, I could become a target."

"He's right! I hadn't thought of it that way before. Shit, Kristina, this could get dangerous."

"Which is why I'm here in the kitchen, baking."

Paige studied me for a long moment. "You're not going to drop it."

I shrugged. No need to implicate her. If things went pear-shaped, then what she didn't know couldn't hurt her.

I hoped.

Chapter Four

"**M**eow."

"I'll be careful, Velma. I promise."

"Meow. Meooooow."

"No, I will not stay in tonight."

"Meeeeooooow."

"I'll be back real quick, and I'm using a cloaking spell. Okay? Happy now?"

"Mrooow."

"Good girl." I scratched behind her ears and she purred, rubbing against my hand. Velma was a worrier. She'd heard me muttering as I got changed into my cat burglar costume. Well, I didn't have a cat burglar costume, but I was dressed in black. Black chucks, black jeans, black long-sleeve T-shirt, black beanie. It wasn't really necessary since I'd be casting a cloaking spell so humans couldn't see me, but I was in 007 mode and I wanted to dress the part. Why? Because tonight I was going to spy on Jodi. She was involved in this somehow. I just knew it. My plans had been momentarily thwarted by Ben, but I hadn't let his words of caution deter me for long.

Once I was home from the shop, I'd prepared dinner, fed Velma, and then headed upstairs for a shower, the whole time plotting and pondering my next move. I needed to find out what Jodi knew. It was doubtful she would tell me anything useful personally, so stealth was my only option.

Dropping a quick kiss on top of Velma's soft head, I headed downstairs and out the front door, pausing on the step to cast my spell. Once done, I hurried down the remaining steps and out onto the footpath. I stopped and waited for a minute. A couple was approaching—the perfect chance to test my spell. Would they see me? I stood to one side and pulled faces. Nothing. They walked right past, oblivious to my presence.

Jodi didn't live far from me, only a couple of streets over. While Redmeadows was quite big, it was also quite small, depending on the circles you moved in. Given that I'd just rendered myself invisible, I couldn't catch a cab, so I set off at a light jog, mindful to slow to a walk when people came near, lest they hear the thud of my footsteps. While my apartment was a standalone, narrow, three-story red brick building, Jodi lived in a multi-level apartment complex.

Out of breath, I stood outside for a few minutes, eyeing the building. Glancing at the time on my phone, I sent up a prayer, hoping I'd timed it right. Paige had found out that Jodi attended Pilate's classes on Monday nights. She should be getting home right about now, and I could follow her all the way into her apartment. If I'd already missed her, then tonight had been a colossal waste of time.

The heavy scent of vanilla and sweat hit my nostrils and I turned. There she was, all flushed and sweaty in her workout gear. As she moved past me, I glided in behind her, careful not to touch her or give her that prickly sensation of someone standing too close, but I also made sure I wasn't so far away that I couldn't slip through the door behind her.

So far, so good. We were in the foyer. I waited while she got her mail, then followed her into the lift, maneuvering myself into the front right-hand corner, away from the panel. She hit the button for the eleventh floor and flipped through her mail while the elevator delivered us smoothly upwards.

With a ping, the doors opened into a long, narrow hallway. She turned left, and I followed all the way to the end. Nice—she had a corner apartment. Again I squeezed in behind her as she unlocked her front door, just before she kicked it closed behind her, flicking the deadbolt and chain in place.

Oh, crap. I hadn't thought about how I was going to get out!

Jodi's apartment was the perfect size, neither too big nor too small. Its open plan had a sleek white kitchen off to one side, a dining area next to it, and a lounge area along with big windows at the front of the building. All of it was decorated like a spread from a magazine. Mostly neutrals, accented with splashes of light blue, with a seashell here and there. Very tasteful. And very different from my eclectic decorating efforts. If I saw something I liked, I'd get it, with little thought about whether it would match what was already in my home. Jodi appeared to have purchased every last item in her apartment with a certain design idea in mind. I kind of envied her that. Her place looked neat, tidy, and well put together.

She dropped the mail onto a side table and crossed to an open door on the far side of the room. Her bedroom. I stopped in the doorway when she started pulling her clothes off, tossing them at the overflowing hamper in the corner on her way to the bathroom. I had no desire to spy on Jodi naked. Quickly stepping back into the lounge, I started to look around in earnest. But now that I was in her living room, ideas failed me.

I wanted proof she knew Rebecca. I wanted a lead that would tell me who Rebecca was and where I could find her. I hadn't stopped to think about what those leads might actually be. Hurrying into the kitchen, I began pulling out drawers, looking for an address book, a diary, a journal, anything that might have the information I needed. Nothing. Just tons of recipe books, but then again, like me, she liked to cook. I had to stop myself from flipping through her recipe books—I'd give her that courtesy at least.

Finding nothing in the kitchen, I shuffled through the mail she'd left by the door. Bills. Junk mail. Nothing exciting or incriminating. I searched the lounge, looking under cushions, skimming through the bookcase. Nothing.

Damn it.

The shower shut off and I crept over to the bedroom door, pressing my back against the wall just outside. I listened as she moved around. It sounded like she was putting clothes on, thank God, otherwise, this whole escapade would have gotten a ton more awkward. She breezed past me in a cloud of vanilla and my nose twitched. Holy shit. Do not sneeze. Do NOT sneeze. I pinched my nose, breathing through my mouth until the urge passed.

Jodi had pulled a bottle of wine from the fridge and was busy pouring herself a glass. I slipped into her bedroom and began quietly opening drawers. Then, on the bedside table, I saw it. A photo of Jodi with another woman. They had their arms around each other. Jodi's blonde head rested against the brunette's. The brunette looked vaguely familiar. Had I seen her at the afternoon tea? Could this be Rebecca? Picking up the frame, I carefully removed the backing. Bingo! Printed in neat handwriting were the words Jodi and Rebecca, summer 2012. Putting the frame back together I slid my phone out of my back pocket to snap a photo. Now I knew what this Rebecca looked like. But if they were friends—close enough friends that Jodi kept a photo of her in her bedroom—there had to be more. A phone number. An address.

Then it hit me. How could I be so dumb? Where else would you keep that sort of thing but on your phone? Duh! I crept out of the bedroom and discovered Jodi now curled up on the sofa with her glass of wine, her phone in her hand as she scrolled through whatever was on her screen. Silently, I crossed and stood behind her, peering over her shoulder at her phone. She was on Facebook, posting updates and commenting on statuses.

Then I saw her like a post by Rebecca Keller. I straightened, then froze when Jodi twisted to look over her shoulder, right at me.

Thank God my spell held, otherwise this would have been incredibly awkward. With a shrug, she returned to her phone. I retreated to the kitchen, pulling myself up onto the counter. I sat and waited. I had no choice; I couldn't slip out of the apartment until Jodi went to sleep. By the grace of God, I'd discovered something useful, but now it was time to get the hell out of dodge.

For two hours, I sat on that kitchen counter waiting for the social media queen to put her damn phone down and go to bed. Geez. I'd promised Velma I wouldn't be long—plus, my concealment spell would start to fade soon. As it was, I'd propped myself up on the floor behind the bench, just in case it wore off while she was still awake.

Finally, the lights went out, and I could hear the bed creak as she climbed beneath the covers. I waited a little longer, listening as she tossed and turned until there was nothing. Creeping across the room, I poked my head around the door. She looked like she was asleep. I wasn't going to poke her to find out.

Back at the front door, I slid the chain off, biting my lip as I tried not to make a sound in the now quiet apartment. The deadbolt clicked, the sound horrifically loud. I froze, listening. Nope—she was still asleep, or simply hadn't heard me.

Gripping the door handle in my sweaty palm, I turned, wincing as that, too, made too much noise for my liking. I slid through the gap in the door and closed it behind me as quietly as I could. I cast a quick spell to make it impossible for anyone to break in despite the door being unlocked. Then I hurried down the corridor, back into the lift, and out into the street, jogging all the way home.

"Meow meow meow!"

"Yes, I know I'm late. My humblest apologies, oh furry one. It couldn't be helped. But I have good news, Velma..." I scooped her up into my arms, nuzzling my face into her neck. "I found out who Rebecca is. Full name: Rebecca Keller and she and Jodi are friends. Good friends, by the looks of it."

With Velma still cradled in my arms, I climbed the stairs to my bedroom, plopping her down on my bed with another quick kiss. Next step? Find out everything I could about Rebecca Keller.

Chapter Five

"Care to explain what you were doing in Jodi O'Flannigan's apartment last night?" Ben stood outside my door, frowning.

"Who said I was?" I bluffed, turning away and leaving him standing on the doorstep.

"She called the police this morning. Thinks someone may have entered her apartment while she was sleeping. She swore her door was deadlocked and chained when she went to bed last night, but when she got up this morning, it was unlocked. She also got the sensation someone was watching her last night. Care to explain that?" He'd followed me into the house and now stood in the kitchen doorway.

"Overactive imagination?" I busied myself making us both coffee. I had no idea how Ben took his and rather than ask—he was a little intimidating in cop mode—I simply made his the way I took mine. White with one.

Holding the mug out to him, I gave him a tentative smile. Of course, Jodi had called the cops. And it had been silly of me to assume Ben didn't have connections with the human police force.

"You can cut the crap, Kristina. I know it was you." He accepted the mug and took a sip. "Your magic was all over the place."

"Oh." Busted. Of course, another witch would know I'd been there. And to be honest, I hadn't thought Jodi would call the police just because she thought she'd locked the front door. Anyway, she'd been perfectly fine. I'd made sure the door was secure.

"I told you we're taking care of this," Ben said. "Sit tight. Keep your nose out of it."

"Sure." I shrugged. I had no intention of doing that, and I was sure he knew it.

"Why don't I believe you?"

"I don't know. Why don't you believe me?"

He shook his head. "You're impossible."

I sipped my coffee, looking at him over the rim. He was as gorgeous as ever, his face freshly shaven, his hair neat. He hadn't run his fingers through it yet. I liked him a bit rough around the edges, with a bit of stubble. Oh, who was I kidding? I liked him full stop.

"What are you thinking about?" Those dark eyes zeroed in on me and I swallowed, drowning in them.

"You really don't want to know," I croaked, clearing my throat.

"Maybe I do." His voice dropped to a deep husky growl and my lady parts tingled. Holy shit. Taking my coffee cup from my hand, he set it on the countertop, placing his next to it. Then he cupped my face in his hands and slowly lowered his head. My eyes drifted closed, the anticipation of his kiss almost killing me.

"Shit," he cursed, and my eyes sprung open.

He released me, stepping away, and I looked on in confusion. Why was he backing down? When he reached into his pocket and took out his buzzing phone, I finally clued in.

"Hoffman," he barked into the phone, running his hand through his hair, much to my delight. "Yeah, I checked it out. No signs of a break-in." He scowled at me, and I realized that whoever was on the other end of the phone was talking about Jodi's intruder. A wave of guilt washed over me. Scaring her hadn't been my intention. I had simply wanted information.

Ben turned and walked into the living room, his voice low as he continued talking on the phone. Picking up my coffee cup, I finished the rest in a long gulp before rinsing the cup and leaving it to drain on the sink.

"I've gotta go," Ben said as he returned. He quickly drained his coffee, rinsed the cup, and set it down next to mine. The simple domesticity of the gesture warmed my heart.

"Stay out of trouble." He brushed his knuckles across my cheek, then turned to go, leaving me in hormonal overload in my kitchen. The brush of his fingers on my skin had triggered a fire in my veins that had also pooled in my belly. It took several deep breaths to get myself back in order, and by then he was gone.

* * *

"I've found out a bit more about Rebecca Keller." Paige plopped her laptop on the bench in Jam's kitchen and angled it so I could see the screen while preparing a batch of inspiration icing to go on the cupcakes cooling on the rack.

"She is quite gorgeous, isn't she?" I admired the young, slim brunette in the chic dress.

"Very. She's married to a man who's quite a bit older than her. Roger Keller. He doesn't do social media, but from what I've been able to find out on Google, he runs a successful consulting business and is very rich. Family money. Here's a picture of the two of them that Rebecca posted."

I looked at the photo of Rebecca with her husband, a little surprised. He was definitely older, and more on the plump side. He had his arm around her as he smiled at the camera. On the other hand, Rebecca's smile didn't reach her eyes. She'd angled herself away from him, one arm crossed over the front of her body. This was not a happy couple.

Or, to be precise, she was not a happy wife. Roger appeared perfectly content.

"How long have they been married?" I asked.

"Four years."

"Tell me about his family money."

"It comes from his mother's family, and she still controls the purse strings. Roger doesn't have full access to the family fortune; it won't be turned over to him until she dies."

"Hmmm. Do you know any more about Jodi and Rebecca? Their friendship?"

"Yes. They were in college together. There's a suggestion that they might have been a couple, but when I was going through the Facebook posts, I didn't see either of them come out and say it. Jodi attended Rebecca's wedding. After that, there weren't as many pictures of them together. Maybe one or two a year."

I blew out a sigh. It wasn't a lot to go on. Maybe Jodi and Rebecca had been a couple until Roger and his money caught Rebecca's attention. Once she'd married him, her friendship with Jodi had drifted. Not unusual—that often happened.

"I wonder what Jodi and Rebecca were fighting about," I said. "Their relationship would have been old news. They wouldn't still be fighting about it, would they? Maybe Rebecca did leave Jodi for Roger, but that was four years ago. And what has that got to do with Ted?"

"Maybe Rebecca was having an affair with Ted?" Paige chimed in.

I looked at her in surprise. That could work. Rebecca didn't look happy in the photo with Roger, so maybe she'd taken a lover. Ted.

"I have to talk to her." It was the only way to get to the truth. Paige and I could be barking up the wrong tree entirely. Rebecca could've been unhappy in the photo because her feet were hurting, for all we knew. I was trying to twist the clues to fit my story, and that just wouldn't do.

"Continue to stalk Rebecca on social media," I instructed Paige, "and let me know when she checks into somewhere public."

"Will do." Paige returned to the front of the shop, taking the laptop with her, while I decorated the cupcakes. My inspiration icing was another favorite with my customers.

Once the baking was finished, I joined the staff out front, helping to clear the tables and stopping to chat with customers. I loved the hands-on aspect of my job, and getting to mingle with my customers was always a thrill. My customer service was one of the things I prided myself on, and it kept regulars coming back time and again.

I was on my way back to the kitchen with a tray of dirty dishes when Paige waved me over. "Rebecca just checked in to the Redmeadows History Museum."

"Excellent. I'll stack these and scoot on over, see if I can catch her."

"What will you say?"

"Probably the truth." I shrugged. "It kinda backfired with Jodi. Snooping in her apartment freaked her out, and I feel bad about that."

"But if Rebecca did it, you'd be tipping her off that you're onto her," Paige argued.

I lifted a shoulder. So what if I did? Maybe she'd do something foolish that would lead the Watcher to her door. Or I could give everything I knew to Ben myself. That would be the sensible thing to do. Grabbing the keys to the van from the hook, I shrugged into my jacket and headed out.

I'd never been a sensible girl.

Thankfully, parking wasn't an issue. The underground garage at the museum was half empty. It'd been a long time since I'd visited the museum—years in fact—but today I didn't have time to meander through the exhibits. I was on a mission.

As I power-walked through the building, I couldn't help but wonder what Rebecca was doing here today. After an hour of practically sprinting through the building, frantically searching for her, it hit me. I hadn't tried the North West Café. Maybe she was there.

Bingo. I recognized Rebecca straight away. She was sitting across the table from a matronly woman. She had her planner spread open in front of her with a pen in one hand and a coffee cup in the other. Some sort of meeting. I waited in line to buy my own coffee, then sat strategically a few tables away, where I could keep Rebecca in view. I'd approach her when the other woman left.

What I hadn't expected was that Rebecca was paranormal. I couldn't tell what she was for sure, but by her glow, especially around her head, I wondered if she were part angel. It had been known to happen—angels and humans getting together and creating Nephilim children.

Two coffees later, they finally finished, and my bladder was ready to burst. The other woman left. Rebecca was beginning to pack up her belongings. I rushed over and slid into the recently vacated chair.

"Oh!" Rebecca gasped, a hand going to her throat.

"Sorry, didn't mean to startle you. I'm not sure if you know me, but I'm Kristina Gates—I own the Jam coffee shop."

"Oh, yes, I've seen you around, I think. Certainly heard of you." A grin tugged at her pink lips.

"Yes, I'm sure Jodi has shared a story or two."

Rebecca's eyes narrowed at the mention of Jodi. "How can I help you?"

"Were you having an affair with Ted McNeil?"

Rebecca's face drained of color, then flushed a furious red. She shot to her feet, shoving her planner into her oversized handbag, and stormed off.

"I'll take that as a yes!" I called after her.

Spinning on her heels, she stalked back to me, her whole body rigid.

"I don't know who told you that, but seriously, it's none of your business." Her voice was as cold as snow on a winter's day.

"It is when I'm being framed for a murder I didn't commit. Sit back down. Let's talk."

She assessed me for a few moments before begrudgingly returning to her seat.

"Here's what I know. You were seen arguing with Jodi at the Quinns' afternoon tea. Then, afterward, you were seen arguing with Ted. Looking through your social media photos, you don't look particularly thrilled to be married to Roger—" I held up my hands in defense. "—although I could be totally wrong. I'm just calling it how I see it. But since it was my cupcake that was poisoned, and my business name being dragged through the mud, you can bet your bottom dollar I'm going to keep digging until I get to the bottom of this."

I'd expected Rebecca to be shocked and horrified at the mention of poison and murder. Instead, she went in a totally different direction.

"How do my photos give me away?" she said. "I'm careful what I post on social media. I have to be, because of Roger's position."

"Let's just say I'm good at reading body language. And yours is very telling."

Her face twisted in a grimace. "I asked Roger for a divorce. He refused. He can only get his hands on the family money if he remains married."

"So you had an affair. To force his hand?"

"Not really. It just sort of happened, Ted and I. I guess he could see I was unhappy, and he started to pay me attention, something Roger stopped doing as soon as we got married. It turned my head."

"Did Roger find out?"

"I don't know. Maybe. A week ago, Ted called it off." Her eyes filled with tears. "I was heartbroken. I love him—loved him. I thought he loved me too, but then out of the blue, he called, said it was over and not to contact him."

Interesting. Did she love him enough to kill him for leaving her? Crazier things had happened.

"I don't know why you think you're a suspect," she continued, wringing her hands. "The Watcher thinks I did it. He says I had motive, that I had the opportunity, and that I was found with Ted's... body."

Holy smoke. Ben had never mentioned any of this to me. I almost snorted—as if he'd divulge such things! It also confirmed that Rebecca was paranormal; she'd never have known about the Watcher otherwise.

"Did you kill him?"

"No. I did not. I loved him. I wanted us to get back together. I was prepared to leave Roger. Even if he wouldn't divorce me, it didn't mean I had to stay in a hateful marriage. That's what we were arguing about. Jodi, Ted, and I. I'd already decided I was leaving Roger. Even if Ted didn't want me, I couldn't stay in the marriage any longer."

"Couldn't you use your powers?" I didn't know for sure whether she had any special abilities, but I hazarded a guess.

She shook her head. "My talent is that I can heal myself and others, but when I do, I absorb the powers of those I heal. I can't cast spells or alter people's thoughts."

"Yet you didn't heal Ted?"

"I tried. He died almost instantly. The Abatwa poison is instantaneous. As soon as it breaks the barrier of your skin, you're dead. And I can't bring back the dead."

Interesting. So Ben had told her about the poison already. I don't know why I felt miffed at that. Maybe because I thought there was a spark between me and Ben, that maybe he'd shared intel with me because of it. Turned out I'd got that all wrong.

"So Jodi was trying to talk you out of leaving Roger?" I asked.

"Jodi was all for me leaving Roger, but she didn't want me getting back together with Ted, either."

"Were you and Jodi a couple? Back in your college days?"

"What?! No! Why would you ask that?"

"Oh, just wondering. Never mind. Go on. So Jodi was all for you leaving Roger but not in favor of you hooking up with Ted."

"She thought Ted was a womanizer. That I'd only been attractive to him because I was married. She seemed to think that he ended things with me because I started making noises about leaving my husband."

"So you confronted Ted with that?"

"Yes." Her chin wobbled and she blew out a breath.

"What did he say?" I leaned forward, elbows on the table. This was better than a soap opera.

"He denied it. He said he'd be delighted if I left Roger, who was clearly using me and had tricked me into a marriage of convenience. But he said he still couldn't be with me, that he couldn't explain yet, but he would once the dust settled."

"What do you think he meant by that?"

"Only one thing I could think of. It had to be business-related. I don't know if he and Roger had a business deal or were proposing one, but that's the only thing I can think of that would derail any plan of Ted's. He lived for his business. He would have done anything to protect it."

"Yeah, I've heard he was pretty cutthroat in the business world."

She nodded. "He is. Or rather, was. He built his business up from nothing. Not with family money, like Roger." The last part came out on a sneer, and I couldn't blame her for being bitter.

"Did Ted talk to you about his business dealings?"

"Some."

"Is there anything he told you that could have relevance to his murder, do you think? If we take you as a suspect off the table, who is left?" I didn't think she'd killed the man. Her aura was clear, for one, and the love and hurt shining in her eyes made my own heart ache in sympathy.

"Well, he did have a meeting with one of his employees that he wasn't looking forward to. Paul Keyes—his Chief Financial Officer. There were some anomalies in an audit Ted had arranged, and he needed to go over the books line by line with Paul. Ted was very upset by the findings."

And the plot thickened. People killed over money all the time.

Thanking Rebecca for her time, I gave her a quick hug before leaving. The poor woman looked a little shaken, and very relieved that I believed her.

Afternoon traffic was heavy getting back to the Jam, but it gave me plenty of time to go over my options. I'd cleared Rebecca as a suspect, and—

grudgingly—Jodi too. To be honest, I'd never thought Jodi had done it, but daydreaming about her being carted away in handcuffs had given me a weird sense of satisfaction. Her aggressive nature had been a thorn in my side ever since she'd decided we were competitors, and therefore enemies. I'd extended the hand of friendship more than once, only to have it slapped away.

Chapter Six

J am was packed when I returned. I stayed after closing to bake more cookies and cakes since we'd almost been wiped out in the afternoon rush. Not that I minded. I preferred to be here, baking for my store, than at home twiddling my thumbs because all my catering clients had canceled.

With three bowls of mix on the go at once, the kitchen was a hive of activity, the spoons swirling around and around while I busied myself preparing the different flavors of icing I'd need for decorating. Once I'd gotten all the mix into the pans and in the oven to bake, I scrubbed the kitchen until it gleamed. We had a five-star food quality rating, and I didn't intend to lose it. By the time I'd finished, it was getting close to midnight. Velma would be worried. And hungry.

After one final walk around the shop to make sure everything was as it should be, I set the alarm and let myself out the back door. My van was parked directly behind the shop. Even though it was just a five-meter walk, there was no street lighting, making it a little spooky.

Another ten minutes and I was home, pulling the van into the single-car garage at the back of my apartment. Solar garden lights lit my path to the back door. I had just put my key in the lock when the door burst open and a dark figure plowed into me. I flew backward, my head hitting the ground with a loud crack. I lay there, dazed, listening to the sound of footsteps running away.

Someone had been in my house.

I scrambled to my feet and put a hand to the large egg on the back of my head. Son of a bitch, it hurt! Looking through the back door, I could see my kitchen in shambles. Oh no. Velma. Oh, please let her be okay! Racing inside, I called for her, my voice frantic.

No response.

Running upstairs, I kept calling, until finally, I heard her. I followed the sounds of her soft, pitiful meows. If he'd hurt her, I'd kill him. I found her locked in the spare room closet. Oh, thank God. I pulled her into my arms and buried my face in her fur, only now aware that I'd been crying silent tears, now that her fur was stuck to my face.

"You okay, girl?" I murmured, stroking her.

"Meow."

She purred, rubbing her head under my chin. She was fine. Not hurt. Blowing out a shuddering breath, I held her as I made my way back downstairs to survey the damage—and to close and lock the back door.

My kitchen was a mess. Every cupboard door hung open. Most of the contents had been dragged out and smashed on the floor. Flour, sugar, milk, and eggs had been strewn around the room, including the ceiling, and I hazarded a guess that I no longer had a single piece of crockery intact. It was in pieces all over the floor.

The lounge had fared slightly better. Maybe he'd only just gotten started in here when I came home. Sitting down on the sofa, since the armchairs had been tipped over, I put Velma on my lap and pulled out my cell phone.

"Watcher Hoffman," barked Ben's voice. "Do you know what time it is?"

"Just after midnight?" I guessed.

"Kristina? Is that you?"

"Yes." To my utter horror, my chin began to wobble and I felt a lump in my throat.

"Is everything okay?"

"Someone…" I choked out, but the rest of the words got stuck in my throat. My eyes flooded with tears, blurring my vision.

"Are you hurt?" His voice was urgent now. I could hear rustling. I must've woken him.

"Only a little bit," I sniffled, forcing the words out.

"Only a—? What the hell? Are you at home?"

"Yes."

"Stay there. Do not move. Do not touch anything. Are the doors locked? Are you safe?"

"Yes."

"I'm on my way. Just hang on, I'm coming."

Words that made my heart sing, although I felt a little embarrassed by the waterworks. Maybe it was the blow to my head and the shock. And the blinding panic that Velma could've been hurt. As if sensing my thoughts, she head-butted my hand, demanding attention, and I sat and stroked her silky fur while waiting for Ben.

I was still sitting there when a car screeched to a halt outside and a pounding started at my front door. Still unable to put Velma down, I carried her with me and opened the door.

"What's happened?" Ben barreled in, kicking the door closed with his boot. Both of his hands came down on my shoulders as he searched my face.

"Meow," Velma protested.

"I'm not going to hurt her." Ben glanced down at my cat, then back at me—then over my head at the overturned furniture in the lounge, and beyond, to the carnage in the kitchen.

"A break-in," he said. "I'll call it in. You sit. You look like a strong wind could knock you over." He guided me back to the lounge and I gratefully sank down, leaning back until my throbbing head rested on the plush back of the sofa. A headache had begun to thrum at my temples now that the adrenaline rush was wearing off.

"A squad car will be here soon. Is anything missing?" Ben asked me once he'd gotten off the phone.

"I'm not sure. Hard to tell in the kitchen. Everything appears to be broken or smeared over the walls and ceiling. I figure he'd just gotten started in here when I got home."

"He was inside when you got home?" Ben squatted in front of me, one hand on my knee, warming me through my jeans.

I nodded. "I was coming in the back door. He must've heard the key in the lock. Just as I was opening the door, he pushed through, knocked me down, and ran away."

"You were hurt in the fall?" Without asking, his hands moved to my head, threading through my hair to examine my scalp. His lips twisted when I winced. "That's quite a lump. Once the patrol turns up, I'm taking you to the hospital for a checkup. You could have a concussion."

"You could heal me," I suggested, but he was already shaking his head.

"Not a head injury. Too risky." I nodded; he was right. With the way my head was throbbing, a little medical attention was a good idea.

A patrol car arrived, lights flashing. Ben let them in, then came back to me.

"I'm taking you to get checked out." He held out a hand to me and I took it, letting him pull me up.

"Meow."

We both glanced at Velma, who I still held clutched to my chest with one arm.

"She can't come to the hospital," Ben said.

"Right." I knew that, but couldn't bring myself to put her down. Ben took her from me and I bit back a protest. "I'm going to put her in your bedroom, okay? I'll make sure the officers don't go in there until we get back."

"Okay."

I let Ben guide me into the passenger seat of his truck, the pounding in my head making my movements slow and sluggish. The ride to the Williams Memorial Hospital was quick and silent. I'd closed my eyes but could feel the heat of Ben's stare each time we stopped at a traffic light. He was worried. So was I. My head hurt like a son of a bitch and I felt sick.

I wouldn't say having a cop with me got me preferential treatment in the emergency room, but I would say I was seen very quickly. It could have been because I had a head injury, though. One that was making me puke. As soon as I'd laid on the gurney, the room had spun, and I'd heaved over the side onto the floor. I was mortified. Tears of pain and embarrassment streamed down my face. The young nurse was wonderful, assuring me it was all okay and that she'd seen worse. She gave me a vomit bag just in case.

My time at the hospital passed in a blur. There were X-rays and scans. The doctors shone lights in my eyes. Ben and the registrar discussed my care. There was no fracture, thank God, but a definite concussion. They wanted to admit me overnight, but I'd insisted on going home. To Velma. The anguish of thinking something had happened to her tonight had broken my heart and I didn't want to be away from her, whether she was hurt or not. Ben finally sighed in resignation and promised he'd stay with me, waking me every hour as instructed. It was going to be a long night.

"Kristina. Wake up." Ben was shaking my shoulder, rousing me from a deep, dreamless sleep. I didn't want to wake up, didn't want to return to the pain, so I dug in deeper, refusing to be roused. "Come on, sweetheart."

Hmmm. I liked the cajoling. That got my attention and I drifted up, somewhere between sleep and wakefulness.

"Babe, open those beautiful eyes for me," Ben said.

Oh, that got me. Struggling to the surface, I blinked. Ben had kept the lights off in my bedroom but the door open, allowing the light from the hallway to spill in.

"There you are." He smiled at me, his face close to mine. I was tucked under the covers, and he was stretched out on top of them, his head propped up on one hand.

"Hey," I croaked, mouth dry.

"Need a drink?" He was already turning away to his side of the bed but returned a second later with a glass in his hand. He held it to my lips, and I took a grateful sip before flopping back against the pillow. My eyes drifted closed. As much as I tried to keep them open, I couldn't.

He chuckled. "Losing you again, eh?" I felt him brush the hair back from my forehead, and then I was out.

"Come on gorgeous, wake up for me."

Why was he waking me up when I'd only just fallen asleep? Holy mother of God, I just wanted some peace. I rolled away, but a hand on my shoulder rolled me flat on my back. "I know you don't want to wake up. That's the whole point, Kristina. The sooner you wake up and talk to me, the sooner you can rest again. I know it sucks, but you have a concussion."

Right. I'd hit my head. The pain was receding at last, but I was still incredibly sleepy. I dragged my eyes open and frowned at him.

"I'm awake," I grumbled.

He grinned at me, a dimple showing in one cheek. How had I never noticed his dimple before? I closed my eyes. Damn, but he was cute.

"Hey, gorgeous girl, open those sexy eyes and give me a smile," the warm, deep voice purred in my ear.

I responded immediately, curling toward him as my eyes fluttered open. Ben stroked my cheek.

"I finally figured it out," he told me.

"Oh?"

"You respond really well to compliments."

"Doesn't every woman?" I smiled, closed my eyes, and went back to sleep.

Then: "You have the most perfect skin." Fingers stroked across my cheek, and I purred. "It's so soft I can't stop myself from touching you. I wonder if it's this soft everywhere?"

My eyes sprang open. Ben was laying by my side, fingers brushing my face. He looked tired. I glanced over his shoulder and saw that dawn was peeking through the curtains.

"Have you been doing this all night?" I asked, frowning.

He stifled a yawn. "I set the alarm on my phone."

"I'm sorry." I felt bad for keeping him from his own sleep.

"Don't be. I volunteered. It's good to have you lucid at last. Velma is relieved, too." He indicated with his head and I glanced down to find my cat snuggled between the two of us.

"You look beat."

"No offense, gorgeous, but so do you. You might have been sleeping, but it wasn't restful." I blushed at being called gorgeous and he chuckled. "I worked out last night that you really like being called gorgeous, beautiful, and sexy."

"What?" I squeaked.

"And you respond really well to dirty talk."

"I do not!"

"Oh, darlin', you so do." He smirked in a knowing way, dropped a kiss on my nose, and closed his eyes. "I'm pretty sure you're through the worst of it. Now get some rest. God knows we both need it. You've kept me up all night, in more ways than one."

I puzzled over his words until his double entendre penetrated my foggy brain and I blushed. Closing my eyes, I decided I'd worry about it later.

Chapter Seven

It had been two days since my break-in. With my concussion gone, I'd finally been able to process the fact that some jerk had broken into my home. It had to be connected with Ted McNeil's murder, surely—although the only people I'd talked to about that were Katherine Quinn and Rebecca Keller. Had they set someone on me? Because whoever had been in my house had definitely been male, dressed in black, with a balaclava covering his face.

Ben confirmed this when they lifted size ten boot prints from my kitchen floor—and the bold-as-monkey-balls clue that had been left behind. Jodi O'Flannigans business card for Flans and Things. It was a poor attempt to cast blame on the woman. The card had been left on the corner of the kitchen counter, neatly placed on top of all the mess. The card itself was clean, with no flour or egg smeared over it. No way it just accidentally fell out of someone's pocket and landed there. It had been dusted for prints and came up clean. Way too fishy for my liking.

My question now was, whose cage had I rattled to elicit this response?

"I can see the wheels turning from here."

Ben's voice startled me, and I jumped. He'd pretty much moved in over the last two days, initially to look after me while I was out of action, but now that had shifted into some sort of protective detail. While I liked to think I could look after myself just fine, the thought that a murderer might be after me was enough to send an icy shiver down my spine. I was very grateful for the protection Ben offered. I wasn't stupid. It didn't hurt that he was easy on the eyes and being near him made my body tingle. Didn't hurt at all.

We hadn't spoken of that first night, of how he'd talked dirty to elicit a response from me. When we'd both finally woken up later that morning, I'd been curled in his arms, safe, and it had felt perfect. And then we'd gone about our daily lives as if nothing had happened. I didn't know what to think.

It was also extremely handy that Ben was a witch. He'd swept away all the destruction with a cleaning spell, repaired all the broken crockery, and set the dishes neatly back on their shelves. Even the ceiling was clean. It was as if it had never happened.

"Well," I turned to find him leaning against the kitchen door frame, watching as I prepared coffee, "I was thinking about our suspects."

"Our suspects?" He raised a brow.

I ignored him. "Before the break-in, I'd only had the chance to talk with Katherine Quinn and Rebecca Keller."

He blew out a breath. "You're not going to let this go, are you?" He moved across the room and sat at the kitchen table.

"Nope. You might as well get used to it. Now, Rebecca Keller confirmed she'd been having an affair with Ted McNeil, but he'd broken it off the week before, with no warning."

"I know about the affair," Ben confirmed.

"Did you know that Ted had called a meeting with his CFO—Paul someone-or-other, I can't recall his name right now—because the books had been audited and something got flagged?"

"I knew the auditors had been at Ted's office at his request, but I don't know the results of the audit."

"What if..." I carried two cups of coffee over to the table, sliding one in front of Ben as I took the seat opposite him. "What if this CFO chap had been embezzling from Ted's company and the audit picked it up? What if he panicked and killed Ted so the truth wouldn't come out?"

"A good theory, but killing Ted wouldn't have achieved that. The audit results would still be the same. Anyone would be able to look at them and work it out—that is, if this Paul guy was embezzling. And killing Ted would put the company under more scrutiny, not less."

"Hmmm." He had a point. And if Paul had been embezzling, wouldn't Ted have fired him on the spot instead of arranging a meeting a week later?

"We need to find out what the audit revealed," I said.

"Already on it. Should hear something back today." Pulling out his cell, Ben called his office. "Really? That much? Paul Keyes. Got it. Yes, please."

I only got Ben's side of the conversation, but it sounded promising. He smiled at the eagerness on my face.

"Yes, okay, you were right. Five hundred thousand dollars is missing from the company accounts. It was taken in smaller amounts from different accounts over a period of time. The Chief Financial Officer, Paul Keyes, hasn't been at work since Ted's murder. He's been calling in sick. I've got his home address." He leveled a stare at me. "Want to come?"

"Yes!" I jumped up, delighted he was including me.

Shaking his head in resignation, he muttered to himself, "I must be crazy."

Paul's townhouse was lavishly decorated, dripping with money and sophistication—unlike the disheveled man who was pacing nervously in front of us. Ben had directed me to sit on the sofa and stay quiet. He sat down beside me, and we both watched Paul for a moment, breathing through our mouths to avoid the stench of a man who had clearly not washed in several days.

Ben cleared his throat. "You know why we're here?"

Paul nodded. "Ted's death."

"His murder," I corrected.

Ben cast me a glance. Shut up.

"That, along with the recent audit Ted conducted," Ben said. "Seems there are some anomalies. Care to explain them?"

"What anomalies? I don't know what you're talking about." Paul was lying through his teeth. He was sweating like a pig. I could see the drops running down his face, and his aura was a very unattractive baby poop green.

"Bullshit," I muttered.

Ben nudged me with his knee. Right. Be quiet. I bit the inside of my cheek to keep my thoughts to myself. If I stuffed this up, Ben wouldn't bring me along again, and I really liked having him by my side, fighting to clear my name. Oh, okay, he was primarily here to solve a murder, but I liked to daydream that he was doing it for me.

"Why did Ted have an audit conducted?" he asked.

"I don't know."

"When was the last time the company had been audited?"

Paul shrugged. "A few years back. We do our own internal audits on a yearly basis."

"Yet for some reason, Ted thought it necessary to engage the services of an audit firm. Was he thinking of selling the business?"

"What? No! Well, I don't think so, anyway. He would have said something to me if that were the case."

"Yet he didn't see fit to tell you about the audit," Ben pointed out. "And you're the Chief Financial Officer. Why do you think that is?"

"I told you, I don't know."

"Have you seen the results of the audit?"

"No. I had a meeting arranged with Ted to go over them, but then he was killed."

Ben was silent for a moment. Knowing I wouldn't be able to help myself, that I'd feel the urge to fill the silence, he squeezed my knee hard. He wanted the silence. Admittedly, it was a good tactic. It felt ominous. Paul wrung his hands, stalking back and forth before sinking into an armchair, then just as quickly jumping to his feet and pacing again.

"I know what was in the audit report, Paul," Ben said.

"You do?" Paul's eyes widened. He stopped and stared down at Ben, who was still seated next to me on the couch, giving the illusion of being totally relaxed.

"Quite a sum of money has gone missing, Paul. Know anything about that?"

"No," Paul squeaked, turning pale.

"I'm having a hard time believing you," Ben said.

Another silence, then Paul folded. "I did it. I stole the money. But I was putting it back! I swear."

"Why were you stealing from your employer, Paul? To pay for this?" Ben gestured around him at the luxury apartment.

"It was a sure thing." Paul hung his head. "I met this guy, and he had all these money-making ideas. I mean, they were brilliant. There was no way they should have failed. Yet they did. I initially borrowed money from the company to bankroll the first invention, and the funds from that would have spearheaded the rest. Then I would have returned what I'd borrowed."

"You met this guy where?"

"At a bar."

"And he just handed over his ideas to you?"

"Well, yeah. They seemed so brilliant." Paul went on to explain crazy invention after crazy invention. I frowned. There was no way any of those ideas would have gotten off the ground. Why couldn't Paul see that?

"So to get your initial buy-in, you stole from your boss," Ben said.

"Yes." Paul sniffed, wiping a hand across his eyes.

"Why didn't you sell this place? Borrow the money?"

"I needed a fast turnaround. Plus, this place is already double mortgaged."

"But that first invention—it failed," Ben pointed out. "Not only did it not make money, but it lost money. So you needed to regroup quickly. You borrowed more from the company account to invest in the next invention, and then the next, and the next. Am I close?"

"Yes. Exactly. And if Ted had found out about the money I borrowed, he would have fired me. I need the job. Need the salary." Paul ran a hand through his hair. "Shit."

"I went over the statement you gave the police after Ted's death." Ben changed the subject, much to my surprise. I glanced at him, but his stony face gave nothing away.

"Oh?" Paul slumped into the armchair once more, only this time he didn't get back up. He looked exhausted.

"Your jacket cuff had blue icing on it. Yet you said you didn't get a chance to go over to the dessert buffet. I was wondering how you came to have icing on your clothing."

"I—I don't know," Paul muttered.

Ben's jaw clenched. "You keep telling me you don't know, but I'm thinking you do. What were you doing at the dessert buffet, Paul? Poisoning the cupcake? Did you think killing Ted would get you off the hook?"

"No! Never! Ted was my friend. I would never hurt him."

"Yet you stole from him."

"From the company. Not from him personally. The company can afford to take the hit, and I was going to pay it all back anyway." Paul exhaled shakily. "No. I did not kill Ted."

"Then how did you get icing on your jacket, Paul?"

Paul closed his eyes, squeezing the bridge of his nose, his face screwed up in concentration. Then his eyes popped open. "I remember. Rebecca gave it to me. I hadn't been eating much. I grazed a little, but to be honest, I could barely keep anything down. Rebecca came up with a cupcake in her hand and gave it to me. She said I could do with some fattening up."

"Did you eat the cupcake?"

Paul shook his head. "I couldn't. Honestly, I thought I might puke."

"What?" I was outraged. No one ever barfed after eating one of my cupcakes. Ben squeezed my knee again. At this rate, I was going to have bruises, but it did the trick. I shut up.

"What did you do with the cupcake, Paul?" Ben demanded. "Throw it out?"

"I just held it for a while. Then Ted came over and we were talking."

"What were you talking about?"

"Just useless stuff. Shooting the breeze. How the Reds are doing this season, that sort of thing."

"What happened next?"

"Ted asked me—" Paul was back to wringing his hands again, and his face was deathly pale. "He asked me if I was going to eat the cupcake. And I said no. And I gave it to him. I gave him the cupcake."

Holy shitballs. Had Paul been the intended victim all along? And what about Rebecca? I'd thought she was innocent, but she'd hand-delivered the cupcake to Paul. The cupcake decorated with the blue icing butterfly. The poisoned one. I was practically vibrating in my seat, my teeth biting into my lip to stop myself from interrogating the man myself. Shit on a stick, I hadn't expected this.

"So Rebecca gave you the cupcake, and you held on to it for a while but didn't eat it," Ben said. "You didn't take a lick or a bite?"

Paul shook his head.

"And then Ted took it from you and ate it?"

Paul nodded. "He took a bite from it as he was walking away. He was saying how the desserts from this chick's coffee shop were always amazing. And then he walked over to the dessert buffet. I guess to see what else was there? I don't know. Oh, shit." Paul wiped tears from his cheeks, his head bowed.

"Thanks for your time, Paul. If you think of anything else, please call me." Ben stood up and proffered a business card. I stood up, wiping my palms on my thighs. "Oh, and don't leave town. I can't say what's going to happen with the embezzlement side of things, but running won't help your case."

Paul nodded, still in his chair, looking shell-shocked. We let ourselves out.

"Oh, my friggin' God!" I said once the elevator doors had closed and we were heading down. "Rebecca poisoned the cupcake to kill Paul! I did not see that coming."

"Don't jump to conclusions," said Ben, ever the voice of reason.

"I'm following the evidence, Watcher."

"Yes, I can see that. But you're just assuming Rebecca poisoned the cupcake. What if someone else gave it to her? What if she was the actual target—only she spied Paul looking all washed out and forlorn and decided to give him the cupcake instead?"

I folded my arms. "Do you think that's what happened?"

"No idea. I'm speculating. But we definitely need to speak with her again. Same with this guy Paul met at the bar. I'm pretty sure he must be a Belphegor. Those ideas he was spouting were utter nonsense, but Belphegors are good at seducing people into thinking they are wonderful ideas that will make them rich."

"So not only do we have Abatwas in Redmeadows now but Belphegors as well?"

"Belphegor's have always been around," Ben said. "They're attracted by people's laziness. A big city like Redmeadows is just ripe for the picking."

Chapter Eight

R oger and Rebecca Keller's house was a mansion. A friggin' mansion. A woman in a maid's uniform answered the door and ushered us into a parlor just off the massive foyer, which was dominated by a grand staircase and a chandelier that sparkled in the light.

I'd never been in a parlor before and was somewhat disappointed. I'd been expecting something opulent, but even though I was sure the antique love seat I was sitting on was probably the real deal, it was still just a sitting room. Ben stayed on his feet, gazing out the front window at the manicured gardens. The parlor was very feminine. Tiny figurines sat on almost every available surface, and I'd decided sitting down was my best option in case I accidentally knocked something over and had to pay for its replacement. Something told me I wouldn't be able to afford that type of bill.

"Watcher, good to see you again." Rebecca Keller glided into the room, elegant in a pale pink pantsuit and white stilettos, with her hair twisted into a bun at the back of her head. She looked like a supermodel. I scowled, feeling decidedly frumpy in comparison. She faltered when she saw me. "Oh. You."

Yeah. How flattering.

"Me," I agreed.

"You two work together?" She looked puzzled. I didn't know how to answer her, so I let Ben field this one.

"Miss Gates is helping me with this case in a consultant capacity," he explained.

"But isn't she a suspect? Surely that isn't ethical?" This Rebecca was not the vulnerable Rebecca I'd spoken to days ago. This Rebecca was as cold as ice, and the way she looked down her nose at me had my hackles rising. Ben shot me a glance, warning me—again—to stay quiet. Ugh. As much as it pained me to do so, I complied.

"Miss Gates is not a suspect," was all he said.

I almost laughed out loud. He didn't have to explain himself to her. She clearly didn't like it, judging by the way her back tensed and her mouth pinched like she'd sucked a lemon.

"Please, have a seat." She indicated a small armchair with curved arms and an embroidered cream-colored fabric opposite her own chair. It looked like a throne. We were on her turf now.

"I'll stand, thanks," Ben said.

Her eyes narrowed, but she didn't argue. I shot Ben a glance. This was awesome. He was good at this.

"Suit yourself." She smoothed the fabric of her pantsuit over her knees and looked up at him.

"What can I do for you Watcher?"

"How well do you know Paul Keyes?"

"Paul Keyes?" She tapped a manicured finger against her pink lips. "I don't think I know a Paul Keyes."

"He seems to know you," Ben replied drolly. "The CFO at Ted's company?"

"Oh! That Paul Keyes. Well, yes, I know of him. I don't really know him, though."

Ben raised an eyebrow. "So you wouldn't say you were on speaking terms with him? If you saw him at a social gathering, he wouldn't be someone you'd mingle with?"

"To be honest, no. Paul may be a CFO, but that's what I call a false rank. He's a glorified accountant, not a CEO or a president."

Geez Louise, her prejudice surprised me. Talk about a status-seeking drama queen. My eyes drilled into her. I was having a hard time reconciling this version of Rebecca with the tearful, heartbroken woman I'd met the other day. Even her aura had changed from a light golden glow to a dark orange tint. Interesting. And confusing. I had no idea what it meant. I glanced up at Ben and found him watching me, a brow arched. Then he turned his attention back to Rebecca.

"So you wouldn't have felt compelled to give Paul a cupcake because he was looking hungry and you thought he needed it?"

"No, of course not." Her eyes darted to the floor for the briefest of moments. She was lying.

"That's not what Paul told us. He's very distraught after Ted's death. He didn't remember all the details straight away, but it's often the case after a couple of days that all sorts of small details start to come back to a person. Who said what, who did what."

"Er." She swallowed. She didn't look so sure of herself now.

"One last chance, Mrs. Keller." Ben's voice had gone hard and sharp. I was glad I wasn't on the receiving end of it. "Did you hand Paul Keyes a cupcake at the afternoon tea you both attended on Sunday?"

Silence filled the room. An ornate grandfather clock in the corner ticked away the seconds.

"Um, let me think." She dragged it out, rubbing her palms on her knees again. "Why, now that you mention it, I think I may have."

"You think?"

"Yes. Yes, I gave him a cupcake." She nodded, hands still rubbing away at her knees. Her aura was all over the place, darkening from the orange of earlier to almost red, then back to a strange yellow. I knew Ben could see it for himself, so I continued to sit quietly and wait. This was fascinating.

"And where did you get the cupcake from?"

"The buffet table." She cast a scathing glance at me and I raised my brows in surprise.

"Did you add anything to the cupcake? Tamper with it in any way?"

"What? No!"

"Are you sure? Because let me caution you right here, Mrs. Keller. Lying to me again isn't going to go well for you. Understand?"

"Perfectly, Watcher." She rallied, straightening her shoulders, her hands now clasped in her lap. The ice queen was back.

"Now that I think about it, the truth is, Watcher, I didn't get the cupcake from the buffet table." Her voice was clear and calm. "Wes Quinn gave it to me. He was carrying two—a yellow one and a blue one. He gave me the blue one and I took it to be polite, but truth be told, Watcher, I had no plans to eat it. Too many carbs. I was about to throw it in the bin when I saw Paul and decided to give it to him."

"You're just remembering this now. Convenient," Ben muttered, his eyes narrowed in anger, but his body radiated a calm that I envied. I was so wound up I wanted to slap the silly woman's face. What made me even angrier was that I wasn't one hundred percent sure she was telling the truth. She'd lied before, and I hadn't picked up on it. This one was a player. I didn't trust her. Not to mention that was two people today who'd said they were going to throw my cupcake in the bin. My teeth clenched until they hurt. Bastards.

"You're sure now that Wes Quinn gave you the cupcake?"

"Yes. I'm positive."

"Any reason he was hand-delivering cupcakes?"

"Well, he joked that he couldn't decide between the yellow and the blue, so he grabbed both, but then realized his hands were full and he couldn't hold his drink."

Pfft. That didn't ring true. If that were the case, he'd have put one of the cupcakes back down on the buffet table, not walk away with it. I was guessing Ben agreed with me, based on the expression on his face.

"I've got what I need for now," he said. "Don't leave town, Mrs. Keller. You're not off the hook yet."

She rose to her feet, a triumphant grin on her face, but Ben halted her with his next words.

"Just so you know, you are on my suspect list. Right at the top. Motive. Opportunity." He ticked the words off on his fingers. "If I find out you're lying to me again, I'll be back with a warrant to search this house, your vehicles, any properties you and your husband own, and your husband's offices. Do we understand each other?"

"Perfectly, Watcher." Sweeping out of the room, her back ramrod straight, she left us to find our own way out.

"I'm gobsmacked," I admitted, sitting in the passenger seat of Ben's truck.

He glanced at me, turning the key in the ignition and easing out into the afternoon traffic. "Why's that?" he asked.

"I could have sworn when I talked to Rebecca before, that she was this sweet, innocent woman. I saw no sign of that woman today. And I'd had no clue she'd lied to me. I didn't have her pegged at all and I thought I did."

"Don't be too hard on yourself. Gotta remember I do this for a living."

"I guess."

"So tell me, my little amateur sleuth—what's next?" he asked teasingly.

I thought for a moment, my mind going over everything we'd learned today. Rebecca had given the cupcake to Paul. Wes had given the cupcake to Rebecca. And Katherine Quinn had said she directed Ted to the cupcake buffet directly. At what point was the cupcake poisoned?

"Well, we definitely need to speak with Wes Quinn," I suggested.

"Definitely. And we can't assume Rebecca isn't on the phone right now warning him. But he can wait. Won't hurt to let him sweat."

"Right." My head was starting to ache, and I absently rubbed my temple. Although my concussion had gone—well, the worst of it—my headache kept returning when I was tired.

Ben looked over at me, frowning. "I'm taking you home. You need to rest."

"I'm fine," I assured him, quickly dropping my hand into my lap.

"Bullshit." He laughed. "You should know better than to lie to me, Kristina."

Busted. "Okay. Yes, I have a headache. A quick nap sounds wonderful. Is that what you wanted to hear?"

"It'll do."

He pulled up in front of my apartment and walked me inside, fussing as he settled me on the sofa. Then he brought a glass of water and painkillers and tucked a throw around me.

"Enough already," I groused in mock irritation. "I'll be fine. I need to go into the shop later. I'll have a quick rest and head in."

"Absolutely not!" he insisted. "Paige has it all under control. Stock levels are okay for now. If you have to bake, bake here."

"How do you know about my stock levels? And how do you know Paige?" I eyed him suspiciously.

"Because I talked with her multiple times when you were out of it and let her know you'd be out of action for a few days."

"Oh." Right. Yes, that made sense.

He grinned. "You're welcome."

"Thank you," I replied automatically, yawning.

"Here." He pushed the glass into one hand and dropped two pills into the other. I swallowed them, and he took the glass out of my hand, nudging my shoulder until I was laying on the sofa.

"Rest. I've got stuff to do at the office. I'll be back later. Stay out of trouble." He dropped a kiss on my forehead and was gone.

I lay for a moment, pondering the kiss and the way he'd been taking care of me. Were we a couple? I had flashes of memory from the night of my attack—he'd woken me continuously, stroking my face and hair, and then I'd found myself curled up against his side in the morning, with his strong arms around me as he slept, equally exhausted from our night of interruptions.

He definitely cared, and there was definitely an attraction. A big, strong, hot, sizzling one. My lips curved into a smile as I slipped into sleep.

Chapter Nine

I was elbow deep in cake mix when the message arrived. I'd never received a message from the Council before, and at first, I didn't know what was happening. The room shook. Then, before my eyes, a parchment appeared in midair, unfurled itself, and a booming voice rang out, "Kristina Esmerelda Gates, you are hereby on probation with the Council. Your involvement in the death of a human and your excessive use of magic on the twenty-second have alerted us that you are not in compliance with Council rules. One more infraction, and we will confiscate your magic and bring you in front of the Council for sentencing!"

The parchment disintegrated in a poof of sparks and smoke. Velma scattered, her claws slipping and scratching as she propelled herself from the room at breakneck speed, clearly terrified.

I stood frozen. What. The. Hell?

Okay, I knew the Council was pissed that I was involved in the cupcake murder, but that wasn't my fault. I hadn't killed Ted, and surely Ben had relayed that to them.

Excessive magic, though? What on earth were they talking about? My heart pounded; I was worried I'd be stripped of magic and tossed in the pokey for things I didn't do! I had to clear my name and get to the bottom of this mess, and fast. Picking up my phone, I shot Ben a message. *Where are you?*

I puzzled over the matter as I returned to my baking, but my concentration was shot. Already I had three large containers stacked atop each other, ready to be delivered to Jam. Glancing at the clock, I knew it was too late to do so today. It was nearing eight-thirty, and Jam would be closed. I'd drop everything off in the morning. My afternoon nap had resulted in a three-hour sleep, and I'd woken in a bit of a panic, knowing I had so much baking to do, but I breathed a little easier on that front now that I had a few batches done.

And now this—the Council hot on my ass for things I didn't do.

My phone beeped and I looked at the screen. A message from Ben. *At your front door.*

A loud knock made me jump, but I couldn't contain a grin. Throwing the door open, I drank in the sight of him, wanting nothing more than to run into his arms and have him hold me. But I hesitated, unsure where we stood. As if reading my mind, he stepped forward and pulled me against his chest, resting his chin on the top of my head. Neither of us spoke, but to be honest, it was bliss. Exactly what I needed. His presence calmed my racing mind, settling the panic that bubbled through my veins at the thought of losing my magic and being locked away.

"Something's happened," he muttered, pulling away long enough to shut the front door.

"I had a message from the Council," I blurted out, heading for the kitchen. "I'm on probation."

"What?"

"Apparently, they're not happy with my involvement in the death of a human, and they're pinging me for excessive use of magic. I haven't used excessive magic, I swear!" To my horror, tears burned my eyes, and a lump formed in my throat. I didn't like to cry, and I especially didn't like to cry in front of Ben.

"Hey." He pulled me back into his arms, hand stroking down my back soothingly. "It must be a misunderstanding. I'll sort it out."

I wiped my eyes with the back of my hand and gave him a watery smile "Gah, I'm usually so much more together than this. I feel like such a wreck."

"You've got a lot going on, and you recently sustained a head injury. You don't have to be strong all the time. You can lean on me."

"I can?" I leaned forward into his arms, giving him my weight.

"You can." He squeezed me tight. "In case you hadn't noticed, Miss Gates, I like you. A lot."

"I like you too," I murmured, lifting my face.

His mouth came down on mine, gentle at first until I opened to him and my tongue snuck out, tasting and reveling in him. He was musk and honey and chocolate—all my favorite things. I couldn't get enough. He groaned into my mouth and it was the most erotic thing ever. Clutching his face between my hands, I kissed him as if my life depended on it. He returned the kiss with a heated passion all his own. One hand cupped my nape while the other spanned my jaw, tilting my head just so, getting me exactly where he wanted me. And exactly where I wanted to be.

"I just thought of something." I was snug in Ben's arms and didn't want to return to the real world. I wasn't ready.

"What?" I frowned.

"After your break-in and this place was trashed? I used my magic to fix it. That may have been the excessive magic the council detected. Not from you. From me. But it was coming from your house, so they assumed..."

"The worst. They assumed the worst without even checking!" While I was relieved we had an answer to the magic problem, I wasn't happy that I'd been judged by the Council without an investigation or the chance to clear my name. They hadn't even waited for Ben to report on the status of Ted's murder.

"I'll get it sorted, don't worry." Ben ran his finger over my cheek and I melted all over again.

I pulled his head down to me and breathed into his mouth, "I'd like you to kiss me again."

I felt him smile. "Oh yeah? That's good because so would I!"

Chapter Ten

atherine Quinn smiled as she opened the door to us the following day.

"Watcher. Kristina. Great to see you both again," she said as she ushered us inside, "though I'm surprised to see you here together."

"Kristina is assisting with the investigation," Ben explained.

She nodded. "Ah. I see. Partners, then."

"Yes. Partners," Ben agreed, although the hot look he gave me had me blushing.

"What can I do for you?" Katherine asked.

"We'd like a word with Wes, if he's available. His office told us he's working from here at the moment?"

"Yes, he's staying with me for a while. He took Teddy's death terribly hard. He hasn't been able to face being alone in his apartment, so he's taken up residence in my guest suite. I'll get him for you." She gestured at a grey sofa. "Please, have a seat."

The Quinn penthouse was decorated with casual elegance. Nothing over the top like the Kellers' home and I felt immediately comfortable here. Sitting next to Ben, I tried to ignore the warmth of his leg pressed against mine. I knew from his smirk that he was well aware of the effect he was having on me. I started to scoot over so we weren't touching, but his arm snuck around my waist and anchored me in place.

"I like you just where you are," he growled and I felt my cheeks heat with another blush.

"He'll be right out." Katherine returned, smiling down at us. "Now, drinks, anyone? Coffee, tea? Something cold?"

"I'm fine, thank you," I managed, tamping down on the desire rioting through my body.

"A water would be great." Ben smiled, bringing his ankle up to rest on the opposite knee.

"Flat or sparkling?"

"Flat is fine."

This time, I scooted two inches left so we weren't touching, and thank the Lord Ben didn't stop me, otherwise, I think we might have disgraced ourselves. I refused to look at him. Instead, I studiously examined the magnificent beach painting hanging over the fireplace.

Katherine passed Ben his water, then seated herself in the armchair at a right angle to him. They started to chat about the weather, but I was too preoccupied with trying not to think about kissing him to join in.

"Guys." Wes Quinn strode into the room. He was a handsome man, although disheveled. His hair was mussed and he clearly hadn't shaved in several days. He wore designer jeans that were torn at the knees and a button-down shirt that was buttoned wrong, and his feet were bare.

I caught Katherine's frown. My own came into play when Wes turned and I examined his face. Flashing across his features, almost like a double-exposed photo, was a dog-like beast. A black, furry face, horns, and pointed ears. Terrifying. I sucked in a breath, surprised. Wes didn't have any shifter DNA, and I wasn't entirely sure what I was seeing was a shifter, anyway. I closed my eyes. When I opened them again, it was just Wes, a belligerent expression on his face. Maybe I was overtired and my imagination was running away with me.

"We just have a few more questions from the afternoon tea you hosted recently, Wes," Ben said. If he'd seen what I saw, he didn't react. "I understand you gave your statement to the officers at the scene, but a few things have come to light and I'd like to clear them up with you if that's okay."

"Sure."

Wes padded to the drinks trolley and poured himself a generous glass of some amber liquid. My guess was whiskey or scotch. Neither appealed to me; I was more of a vodka girl. He slouched into the armchair opposite his mother and eyeballed me.

"Why are you here?" It was directed at me with a sneer.

"Wes!" his mother admonished.

"She's with me." No more warmth in Ben's voice. Just steel. This was going to be interesting.

Wes looked at me for another minute, as if trying to stare me down. I returned his gaze. No way was I going to let him intimidate me. He relented, his eyes dropping to his glass as he muttered, "Go ahead, then. Ask away."

"Tell me about the cupcakes you took from the dessert buffet."

"You expect me to remember what I ate?" he said in a condescending tone.

Ben didn't blink. "Did you eat them?"

"What sort of question is that?"

"A serious one. Another witness reported seeing you holding a blue cupcake and a yellow cupcake. Why take two at once?"

Wes was silent for a moment. "I was getting one for someone else."

"Who?"

The silence in the room was heavy. I caught Katherine frowning at her son. Was she unhappy with his behavior? I would be if he were my son. I turned my attention back to him. He was swirling his drink in his glass, his face sullen.

"Answer the question, Wes," Ben prompted.

"I can't believe we're sitting here talking about damn cupcakes when my best friend has just been murdered!" Anger was his defense. Jumping to his feet, he stormed to the fireplace, his back to us. I could hear him dragging in deep breaths.

"Ted McNeil was poisoned by a cupcake at the party," Ben told him.

Wes whirled, pointing an accusing finger at me. "Then arrest her! She's the bitch who made them!"

Katherine sprang to her feet, her face distressed. "Wesley Quinn! You apologize this instant!"

"Miss Gates is not a suspect."

"Why the hell not?" Wes was a very angry man. I was sure it was real hatred I saw blazing from his eyes. Why would he hate me? I barely knew him. I dealt with Katherine when it came to catering arrangements, but beyond that, we didn't move in the same circles and definitely weren't friends. His hatred was alarming.

Ben was on the alert but remained on the couch. "I suggest you calm down and take a seat."

Wes eyeballed him, then came to some sort of decision. Rearing back his arm, he threw his glass at me. I watched in horror as it flew through the air, almost as if in slow motion, the contents rising to the top of the glass and over, to splash across the carpet and table between us. Ben's hand reached out and caught the glass in front of my face. Everyone froze.

"That was a very, very, stupid move," Ben ground out between gritted teeth.

He placed the glass on the coffee table in front of us and rose to his feet, one hand sending a blast of magic across the room. Wes staggered back as the magic hit him, wrapping his wrists in magical restraints.

"Wesley Quinn, you are under arrest for assault," Ben said, his face an angry mask as he moved like lightning to Wes's side.

"What?" Wes and Katherine spoke at once.

"Ben," I cautioned. I didn't want him doing this for me. There was obviously something more going on with Wes, and I didn't want Ben's over-protective tendencies getting in the way.

"If I hadn't caught that glass, he would have inflicted serious injury on you."

"But you caught it. And I'm okay," I soothed, standing up and coming to his side, placing what I hoped was a calming hand on his arm. "You don't need to arrest him, do you? Maybe let him off with a warning?"

"He's sorry!" Katherine cut in. "It's just been such an awful time for him. He and Teddy were so close and—well, as you can see, he's not coping."

Tears filled Katherine's eyes, and my heart went out to her. Ben looked from her to Wes and to me. With a resigned shake of his head, he released the cuffs.

"First and only warning, Quinn. You curb that temper and learn some manners."

Wes rubbed at his wrists, and without a word, he stalked out of the room.

"We'll come back tomorrow," Ben said to Katherine. "We're not done here, but he needs to sober up."

She nodded, her cheeks flushed. "I'm so sorry," she whispered to me, a hand on my arm as we made our way to the door.

"It's okay. I wasn't hurt, but I have to say he doesn't appear to like me much."

"I'll come back tomorrow alone, or he can come to the office," Ben said. "Either way, I need to speak with him. And I won't have Kristina threatened in that way."

Anger still radiated from Ben. I reached down, entwining my fingers with his. I didn't care if Katherine saw.

"Yes, Watcher," Katherine said. "I'll make sure he's sober, even if it means getting rid of every drop of alcohol in the apartment."

The door closed behind us and we waited for the lift in silence. When it finally arrived, we stepped inside and Ben punched the button for the ground floor. The elevator jerked, then began its downward descent. To my surprise, Ben reached for me, cupping my face in his hands he crushed my mouth to his.

I was breathless and disheveled when the doors opened on the ground floor. Straightening my clothes, I stepped out of the elevator, avoiding the gaze of the couple waiting to get in. Ben walked in step with me, and this time he threaded his fingers with mine.

I glanced at him and he shrugged, his lips curling in a smile. "What? I like it! And I needed something to distract me, or I would have gone back upstairs and punched his damn lights out."

Chapter Eleven

"**K**ristina? You're not going to believe who's asking to see you." Paige stuck her head around the kitchen door, her face incredulous.

I slid the tray of cookies into the oven and set the timer. "Who?" I asked, wiping my hands on my apron and beginning preparations for my coffee cake.

"Jodi friggin' O'Flannigan, that's who."

I froze. Jodi was in my shop and asking to see me? Wonders would never cease. Untying my apron, I tossed it on the workbench and stood next to Paige, peeking around her to spy on Jodi. Yup, there she was, sitting at a table near the back, drumming her fingers on the tabletop and looking anxious.

"I wonder what she wants?"

Paige gave me a nudge. "Only one way to find out."

Weaving through the customers in the shop, I stopped to say hello to one or two before sliding into the empty seat opposite Jodi.

"Hey. I hear you wanted to see me," I said.

Jodi looked terrible. Her face was pale, she had dark shadows under her eyes, and her hair looked like it hadn't been washed—or seen a brush—in days.

"Yeah. Thanks." She cleared her throat. "Look, I know you and I haven't always seen eye to eye on things, and I know it's mostly my fault. I'm too competitive for my own good." Her eyes darted away and then back. "But with what's happened with Ted, well..."

Tears filled her eyes and I had to admit, I was taken aback. I hadn't expected this. I reached out a hand and patted her arm awkwardly.

"Anyway, I just wanted to clear the air. There are a couple of things I think you should know." She squirmed in her seat and her cheeks flushed, then paled again.

"Just spit it out, Jodi." I leaned back in my seat and waited. Whatever it was it had to be good. She was worked up into knots over it.

"I stole your coffee cake recipe," she blurted out, then promptly buried her face in her hands.

"Okay." I shrugged. Again, that wasn't what I had been expecting, and it wasn't a big deal. What made my coffee cake unique was my magic, not the recipe itself. I imagined she'd been trying to replicate the adrenaline kick my coffee cake delivered and had failed. Frequently. I bit my lip to stop a smile.

"I'm sorry," she whispered.

"Apology accepted."

She looked at me in shock. "You aren't angry?"

"No. You didn't have to steal it, Jodi. If you wanted a copy, all you had to do was ask." I could afford to be generous. I still felt bad that I'd scared her when I'd ghosted into her apartment.

"Oh."

"Was there anything else?"

"Well, I kinda wanted to talk to you about Ted's death and stuff."

"Okay, sure. Wanna grab a coffee first? And maybe a cookie?" I signaled Paige, who was keeping an eye on us from behind the counter.

"I can't understand why you're being so nice to me when I've been nothing but awful to you," Jodi said.

"We're two different people who view life in very different ways, that's all. You said so yourself. You're competitive, whereas I believe there is enough for everyone. It doesn't have to be you or me. We can both run a successful business without resorting to..." I trailed off. She'd stolen a recipe from me to try to replicate it and hurt my business. That wasn't a nice thing to do, and judging by the state of her, it had been playing on her mind for a long time, the guilt eating her up.

If I could let her off the hook and tell her about the magic, I would have, but that was the number one Council rule: No telling humans about magic. I'd had to petition the council to be allowed to use magic in my baking, and they had strict policies about what I was and wasn't allowed to do. No love potions. No taking away free will. I used what I called fluffy magic. Feel-good magic, like my inspiration icing and my confidence cookies, and my adrenaline coffee cake. So it didn't matter if Jodi stole my recipes or if I gave them to her. She'd never create exactly the same cakes, biscuits, and brownies as me. No matter how hard she tried.

Paige brought over our coffee and two confidence cookies. I figured Jodi could use the boost.

"Okay, so you wanted to talk about Ted. You had a catering contract with him, so I assume you knew him reasonably well?" I prompted.

Jodi took a sip of her coffee, then nibbled on her cookie, nodding her head. "Yes, I knew him pretty well. He's given me a lot of contacts in the business world. My contract with him really opened some doors for me and my business got a huge boost."

"That's excellent." I nodded, encouraging her to continue.

"His death was so unexpected." Yes, well, that was often the case with murder, but I remained silent. Jodi went on: "I guess you know about Rebecca? I mean, I heard you've been working with Detective Hoffman on the case..."

"I'll level with you, Jodi," I cut in. "I was snooping around on my own first. My reputation was taking a hit, and even though I didn't kill Ted, no one else knew that. You understand what bad publicity can do to a small business, right?"

"Yes." She looked away, unable to meet my eyes. Oh, yeah—she'd been helping perpetuate those rumors.

"I figured out you knew Rebecca, and that Rebecca knew Ted in a very intimate way."

"Yes," Jodi said. "Yes, she did."

I wasn't prepared to lay it out for her. I had a feeling Jodi had something more to tell me, so I shut up and waited for her to speak again.

"Rebecca and Ted had been seeing each other for about a year. They were so in love." Jodi sighed. "Rebecca knew Roger would never divorce her, but she was prepared to leave anyway, just so she could be with Ted without having to sneak around."

"How did Ted feel about that?"

"He was all for it. Marriage wasn't important to him, but sharing Rebecca, even though she and Roger were no longer having sex, didn't sit well with Ted. He wanted her to leave Roger, and it took Rebecca a long time to work up the courage."

"Right. So she told Roger she was leaving?"

"Well, no. It didn't get that far. Ted and Rebecca were finally on the same page, and then boom, Ted breaks it off with her. On the phone. He refused to see her face to face, had security turn her away when she showed up at his office and his home. He cut off all contact. She was devastated."

"I can imagine."

"But since then, Rebecca has changed. She's become cold and bitter and nasty." Jodi shook her head. "She's nothing like the Rebecca I knew, and I can't believe the change in her in such a short time."

"Do you think she killed Ted?"

"Initially, I said there was no way on this earth that she could have killed him. She loved him so much. But lately, her behavior? I'm not so sure. He hurt her. Rejected her. Now I can't help but think maybe she retaliated." Jodi's voice was barely a whisper.

"Have you asked her?"

"She won't see me. Won't answer my calls or text messages. We were best friends, and now she's cut me off like I'm nothing."

"Like what Ted did to her."

"I guess."

"What about Roger in all of this? Did he know his wife was having an affair?" It seemed to me in this bizarre love triangle that Roger should be the number one suspect. He refused to divorce his wife and found out she was about to leave him for another man anyway. What husband in that situation wouldn't want to get rid of that man?

"I'm not sure if Roger knew or not," Jodi said. "Rebecca was discreet. She didn't want to damage Roger's reputation, or Ted's, or her own. But…"

"But?"

"Roger's face. At the party. When he saw Ted there, he was surprised and angry. But when he noticed me looking, it was like a shutter came down. His face revealed nothing."

"Roger was at the party?" I said.

"Just briefly, at the beginning. He left after he saw Ted. I saw him leave."

"Did he speak with anyone?" I questioned. "Why did he leave Rebecca behind?"

"They arrived separately. That's the argument I got into with Rebecca. She was in a panic because

Roger had turned up and she wasn't expecting him to, but she was also thrilled that Ted was there because she hoped to corner him and have it out with him about why he broke up with her. And try and talk him out of it, of course."

I shook my head. "I'm sorry, I'm not clear. Why did you argue with Rebecca?"

"I wanted her to stop all the sneaking around and just tell her husband the truth. She refused. She wanted to talk Ted around first, but I thought she stood a better chance of winning Ted back if she actually left her husband first."

Sound advice. I'd probably do the same, although I'd never condone a married friend having an affair in the first place. Anyone that unhappy should just get out instead.

"Back to Roger," I said. "So he, what? Turned up, saw Ted, and left?"

"Basically," Jodi confirmed.

"And you didn't see him speaking with anyone else?"

"He stopped for a brief word with Wes Quinn on his way out. That was all."

Wes Quinn. Was he really the grieving friend he portrayed himself to be, or was he involved in all of this somehow? His dislike of me seemed disproportionate and I couldn't help but wonder if there was more to it. Or maybe that was my ego talking—and my willingness to paint him as the villain, just because I couldn't deal with the fact that someone didn't like me.

"Thanks for dropping by, Jodi. That took a lot of guts."

She shrugged, giving me a tentative smile. "I'm sorry for all the trouble I've caused you over the years. I'm not proud of my behavior."

"Apology accepted. Again. And thanks for all the inside info. It helps. I'll chat with the Watcher and see what he makes of it."

Jodi frowned. "The Watcher?"

"Detective Hoffman," I bluffed, acting as if she'd misheard me. "The cop who's investigating the murder?"

"Oh, yeah. He's gorgeous," she breathed.

"He sure is." I winked, then saw her out of the shop, watching as she walked away. I wondered if Rebecca had been influencing Jodi all these years. She claimed she didn't have the ability, but for Jodi to suddenly have a conscience and do a one-eighty—the timing was suspicious.

Chapter Twelve

"I found out something interesting today." Ben swirled the red wine in his glass and eyed me over the top.

"Oh?" I took a sip of my own drink and waited.

"Roger Keller is a Belphegor."

"Oh my God! Really? Do you think he's the same one who got in Paul's ear?"

"Could be. I need to go back and show Paul a photo, but this is all linked, it seems like too much of a coincidence for it not to be."

"And Rebecca is a Nephilim," I told him about Jodi's visit to the shop and everything she'd told me about Rebecca, Roger, and Ted—and that I had suspicions Rebecca had been influencing Jodi's behavior.

"That could have been Roger," Ben pointed out. "Enticing her to steal from you, to demolish you as her competition through nefarious ways. That sounds like the influence of a Belphegor."

"You could be right. I wonder why?" I thought about it for a minute. "What if Rebecca and Roger planned all this, but they didn't expect Ted to die? What if Rebecca was meant to heal him and absorb his powers?"

"Good theory, but Ted was human. He didn't have any powers," Ben said. "But I agree there is more to the relationship—like why Ted suddenly ended it. If he really was in love with her, wouldn't he have fought for her? He was a shrewd businessman. I doubt he would have been played by her."

"Maybe she was played by him? Maybe he got what he needed from her and, boom, relationship over."

Ben nodded in agreement, reaching across the table for my hand. We'd stayed in tonight. He'd ordered pizza, and it was the most romantic date I'd had in a long time. Not that I had a lot of dates. I didn't date humans. It was too difficult to keep my magic hidden, and most of the paranormals I met refused to date a hybrid. Ben didn't care, and it warmed my heart. I was falling for the guy, and hard.

The buzzing of his phone broke the mood.

"Hoffman." Pushing back his chair, he left the kitchen, and I could hear him walking back and forth in the hallway. Ben liked to walk and talk. I'd never seen him just sit and answer his phone. He liked to be in motion.

"Damn," he cursed. "I'll be right there." Returning to the kitchen, he gave me an apologetic kiss. "Sorry, babe, there's been a kidnapping. I've gotta go. She's a teenage were, and they think she's been taken by a rival pack. I've got to get this under control before any blood is shed. And to stop an underage mating."

"How awful! I hope you find her quickly."

Ben let himself out and I began clearing up after our meal.

A couple of minutes passed before I heard footsteps behind me again. I smiled and said, "Forget something?"

I wasn't expecting the funny-smelling rag that pressed against my nose and mouth. I dropped the dishes and wine glass, heard the glass break, and saw the red wine splash across the floor. I tried to call out, but the rag muffled my voice, and when I tried to suck in a breath, all I got was the strange chemical smell from the rag. My vision started to blur and my knees buckled. Whoever was behind me caught me, a hard arm around my waist, while the rag remained clamped to my face until I passed out.

When I came to, I was tied to a chair and greeted with the sight of Rebecca and Wes making out. What the hell? I blinked a couple of times to make sure I wasn't hallucinating, but yeah—Rebecca was lip-locked with Wes, whose image was flickering between black beast and human.

"Ah, she's awake." Wes dragged his mouth from Rebecca's and turned to study me. We were in some sort of large, empty building. Maybe an old warehouse or giant shed. It was cold and damp, and I had the feeling I wasn't meant to leave this place. Ever.

"What's going on?" I demanded, eyeing the pair.

Rebecca smoothed her Chanel suit over her hips and sneered at me. "Stupid witch fae who doesn't even know her own powers."

"What are you talking about?" My head was foggy with whatever they'd used to drug me. I was having a hard time computing the fact that these two were sucking face. What about Ted? Rebecca's lover and Wes's best friend?

Rebecca saw my confusion and laughed, her head thrown back. "Look at her face, darling. She has no clue."

"Allow me to explain it to you." Wes walked around my chair, eyeing me up and down. "It's the least we can do."

"Why is your face all funny?" His features wouldn't stop switching from crazy dog beast to human.

"Only a hybrid of a witch and a fae can see my true form. I thought I'd gotten rid of them all, but then you turned up. Quite unexpected. I played it cool, hoping to deflect the attention elsewhere, but you wouldn't quit. You were like a dog at a bone, always pushing, pushing, pushing."

"What are you talking about?" I demanded.

"I'm a shadow shifter. Heard of us?"

I scanned my memory. Shadow shifter. Shadow shifter. "You inhabit the body of a host because your true form cannot exist in the mortal realm."

"Very good. Do you know the rest?"

"There's more?"

Wes offered a twisted smile. "A human body can only sustain my possession for a few years before the vessel—well, it pretty much disintegrates. So every five years, I need to jump to a different body. If I keep doing this, it also allows me to use my true shifter form every now and then, as long as I keep to the shadows."

"You're Ted," I realized. That was why Wes had changed—because he was no longer Wes. The shadow shifter had occupied Ted's body before moving into Wes.

"Why kill Ted?" I asked.

"Ted's consciousness died the minute I entered his body. But whenever I leave a host, I like to play games and kill the flesh in different ways. This time it was Abatwa poison. A nice touch, I thought."

I nodded toward Rebecca. "And what does she have to do with all this?"

Wes shrugged. "She's just a means to an end."

Rebecca shrieked at him in outrage. "What the hell, Teddy?"

"Oh, come now, you're in this for your own interests. Don't think you fooled me for one second. I used you to monitor Roger, sneaky Belphegor that he is. You used me for sex because we both know he can't get it up, and you wanted to steal good old Wes's shifter powers. Don't pretend for one second it was love."

"But Wes isn't a shifter," I protested.

"And didn't the Quinn family do an excellent job of keeping that secret? Imagine my surprise when I wounded Wes and Rebecca healed him, only to discover...nothing. Human. Of course, I needed him to be human to possess his body, but we'd thought him a shifter. Cunning bastards."

"Wait. What? So you hurt Wes with the intention that she heals him and steals his powers, then when he was helpless, you were going to take over his body?"

"Got it in one, babycakes. Knew you were a smart cookie."

Rebecca moved into my line of vision, brushing dust from her skirt. "Of course I got the raw end of the deal on both accounts. Roger trapped me into an unbreakable marriage deal. Wes gypped me of his were powers. We had to rally. To keep my own powers, I need to consume others. You are our next best option. Teddy wants you out of the equation, and I need to feed."

"Stop calling me Teddy. It's Wes now," Wes grumbled at her.

"And Roger didn't guess any of this?" I asked. "The affair? It was him, wasn't it, messing with Jodi?"

"Oh, yes, he was playing with her. He does that from time to time." Rebecca shrugged. "We had to step up our plan because you're right, Roger was onto us. He knew about the affair—I mean, when you come home smelling of sex, it's a dead giveaway, right?"

"And he didn't care?"

Rebecca shook her head. "Not about that. Roger has his own plans, and while he didn't care about the affair, per se, he doesn't like to be made a fool of. Roger got in Wes's ear, tricked him into a couple of bad deals, lost us a fortune. When we realized what had happened, we had to act fast."

I looked at Wes. "Was it you who broke into my home? Knocked me down?"

Wes winked at me. "I needed you to back off. I couldn't have you blowing my cover to the Watcher and the Council. It was a piss-poor attempt, I admit." He glanced at Rebecca for a moment, then turned his attention back to me. "Time for talking is over, sugar plum." Wes grinned, tossing a knife over and over in his hand. "Not that this isn't fun chatting and all, but things to do, places to see."

"Wait!" I shouted, my heart thundering in my chest. I'd been so caught up in getting the truth out of them that I'd allowed myself to forget about the perilous situation I was in. "Tell me one more thing."

"What is it?" Wes sighed, standing behind me and caressing my neck with the knife.

"Who poisoned my cupcake?"

Wes barked out a laugh. "I dropped a minute trace of Abatwa poison on the cupcake I'd taken a bite out of, then I poisoned myself." He moved to stand in front of me, clearly pleased with himself.

"How did you get the poison?"

"That's two questions. Time's up, precious!" Before I could react, Wes drove the knife into my stomach. I screamed. The white-hot pain as the blade cut through flesh, muscle, and organs was excruciating. He pulled the knife out, watching as my blood dripped from the blade onto the floor.

"You want to feed?" he asked Rebecca. "Then feed."

I tried to contain the groan that tore out of me. The pain was almost unbearable. I was losing blood fast, knew I was dying. I tried to collect myself, tried to use my own magic, but I needed my hands. They were tied behind me and covered with something that bound my magic.

Rebecca was in front of me now. With her hands above my wound, she sent her own magic into me. The bleeding stopped and my wound began to heal, but with it, I could feel my magic being leached from me. I could see it as it flowed from my body to her hands. I was getting weaker by the second, knew that when she took the last drop, I'd be dead.

"Stop!" A blast of light shot across the room, knocking Rebecca away from me. She fell onto her ass and slid a couple of feet on the filthy floor.

"Get away from her!"

Ben. Thank you, Lord, I threw up a prayer.

Rebecca scrambled to her feet, outrage written on her face. Rather than go for Ben, she lunged at me, toppling my chair backward. I went down with her straddling me, her hands around my throat as she continued draining my magic. Each squeeze of her hands choked me; each wave of her magic healed me—and stole from me. Crafty bitch had done this before.

I could hear Ben and Wes fighting, could make out flashes of magic behind my closed eyelids. I heard the thud of flesh hitting the floor and prayed that it wasn't Ben who'd been defeated. I was weak, so weak that drawing a breath hurt. Rebecca was pulling my magic from me so hard that she almost had my soul, and I knew my time on this earth was almost up. Ben hadn't been fast enough.

Then her weight was gone. I heard her squeal as she was thrown through the air.

"Hold on," Ben told me, crouching by my side and touching my face. "You hold on. Don't stop fighting, Kristina. You hear me? Fight it!"

And then he was gone. The scuffling wasn't so loud now, but that could be because my hearing was going. I was cold, as cold as ice, and everything was black. I turned my head in the direction I thought they were, but couldn't see a thing—only the darkness, waiting to claim me.

"Don't you dare." Ben was back, skidding to his knees by my side. His hot mouth landed on mine. Strong fingers on my jaw forced my mouth open. Warmth flowed from his mouth to mine and a blissful nirvana cascaded down my throat. My magic. He was returning my magic that Rebecca had stolen. The way it tore through me, happy to be back, was overwhelming. It also stung like a bitch. Finally, Ben lifted his head, his worried face looking down at me.

"I thought I'd lost you," he said, voice gruff and eyes glassy.

My own filled with tears that trickled down my temples and into my hair. "I did, too, just for a minute."

Wiping my tears away, Ben righted the chair and freed me, pulling me into his arms and holding me like he'd never let me go. I wrapped my own arms around his waist and held on equally tight.

"Let's get out of here," he said.

"What about them?" I nodded at the bodies of Wes and Rebecca, unmoving on the dirty floor.

"The Council knows. They'll send Cleaners. My job is done." He swept me up into his arms, even though I protested that I could walk. "Humor me." So I did. Wrapping my arms around his neck and burying my face in his shoulder, I let him carry me from the building that would have witnessed my death and settle me into the passenger seat of his car.

"I love you." He clasped my face in his hands and kissed me tenderly. "Call me crazy, but tonight, when I thought I'd lose you, all I could think of was how much I love you. I told myself that if we got through this...I'd tell you. Even if it is too soon. I don't care. I love you."

I smiled up at him. "I love you, too."

The drive home passed in a blur, and the long night of love-making went all too quickly. Before I knew it, we were sitting at my kitchen table once more, silly, sated grins on our faces, when the house shook and a parchment appeared in front of me.

The Council. Now what?

"Kristina Esmerelda Gates, your probation is hereby lifted. You have been cleared in all matters relating to the death of the human Ted McNeil and any use of excessive magic." Another display of sparks and smoke and the parchment disappeared into thin air.

Ben hugged me. "Congratulations."

"Thank you." I was shell-shocked. Such a lot had happened. I'd been accused of murder, cleared of murder, and almost murdered. And I'd found the love of my life. I couldn't wait to see what next week would bring!

What's next?

I hope you enjoyed Cupcakes & Curses. This novella is a peek into my paranormal cozy mystery style. While I have no plans to continue Kristina and Ben's story, I do have a clumsy human, a ghost sidekick, and a talking cat who you are going to love - so make sure you stick around for the Ghost Detective Series. Keep reading for a small snippet.

Many thanks for your support!

~ Jane Hinchey

Ghost Mortem

Whoever said that ghosts exist must be out of their mind.

Oh, wait. That was me. I said that. If you'd told me yesterday that ghosts were real I would have smiled, nodded, and called a shrink to fix your deluded little mind. Now it's my turn to question my sanity when the ghost of my best friend turns up in my apartment. Was it the tequila shots the night before causing this apparition? Or one too many bumps to the head — let's face it, clumsy is my middle name, it really wouldn't surprise me if I'd done some irreparable damage to my grey matter over the years.

Now I have to accept that the paranormal does, in fact, exist. But sadly, my ghost friend is lacking something besides his body. His memory. He doesn't know how he died but suspects foul play and he wants my help to find his killer. I can't refuse, I'm a sucker for a good mystery and the chance to bring my friend's killer to justice is too good to pass up.

Surprises abound as I discover a secret talent for sleuthing, not to mention an unexpected inheritance of a talking cat among other things. But the biggest problem of all? Captain Cowboy Hot Pants, or as he likes to be called, Detective Kade Galloway of the Firefly Bay PD. He's one smokin' cop, but my distrust of the police runs deep, and despite his assurances that he's here to help can I really trust him, or is his offer of assistance designed to keep me from discovering the truth? I guess I'll find out when death comes knocking on my door.

Join Audrey Fitzgerald in the Ghost Detective series, a paranormal cozy mystery featuring a cat, a ghost, and a murder to solve.

Get your copy of Ghost Mortem here: www.JaneHinchey.com/ghost-mortem

About the Author

J ane Hinchey is an Aussie author who loves to write cozy mysteries with plenty of laughs and mayhem along the way – who says murder can't be fun? Her bestselling Ghost Detective series combines all of this into an intriguing melting pot of paranormal danger, fast-paced action, and plenty of tongue-in-cheek snarky humor.

Jane lives in the mortal realm with her non-paranormal man, two cats whose paranormal status is yet to be determined (she did catch them trying to open a portal in the kitchen that one time), and a turtle named Squirt (who is massive!).

Sometimes, when the supernatural chaos calls for a different kind of story, she writes under the name Zahra Stone, where the characters you meet are as sexy as they are deadly.

Connect with Jane at:

Website and newsletter - www.janehinchey.com

Facebook –

www.facebook.com/janehincheyauthor

VIP readers group -

www.janehinchey.com/littledevils